I0780153

Pete & Gwendoline Grew Up: Season One.

J.S. Thompson

For Lonah.

Lonah Celeste Harris

1937-2010

Adult Story Time Publishing LLC.

©2025 All Rights Reserved.

ISBN:978-1-961156-18-0

www.JSTheartist.com

Episode One ...

Son of a Preacher Man.

I

The "Red River County Fair" was the pinnacle of summer in Fargo, North Dakota. An entire week where the whole city is all but shut down for the sake of fighting through crowds to overindulge in unnecessarily fried foods and expensive-cheap beer. The classic car show and robust scenery of butter sculptures and rotund hogs at the 4H exhibit drew in the masses as well.

As 1985's version of the county fair was ending, bittersweet reality shifted; the adults had to act like grown-ups again, and all of the soon-to-be-freshman at North Dakota State had to start growing up and learn how to be adults. Amid the "last hurrah" energy pulsating throughout the fair going Fargonauts on that climactic final Saturday, sat one young co-ed named Kerry Panneli. Sticky and sweating in an out-of-order cotton candy booth, Kerry was desperate for the fair to end.

Kerry Panneli was a farmer-preacher's daughter from Caledonia, Wisconsin. Kerry's upbringing was simple, structured and sheltered. Her life on the farm was God, family, "chorin'," then school, in that order. If she had any free time, her father felt that time should be spent either praying or helping somebody that doesn't have enough free time of their own. "Havin' fun ain't gonna get 'cha any closer to heaven," was his favorite mantra.

Kerry had never ventured anywhere outside the radius of being known as "Pastor John's Daughter" before. She felt college to be the perfect opportunity to drop the moniker. She was starting as a freshman at NDSU the following Monday; however, she left home early for a job at the county fair to earn a few extra bucks, as well as an extra week of freedom. As happy as the idea of freedom made her, by Saturday, Kerry was over being relegated to a tiny box, spinning sugar and watching people love the lives they were living.

As the five o'clock sunrays pierced through Kerry's plexiglass cage, she sat sweltering and annoyed, waiting for both her shift to end, and for someone to come and fix the "G.D." cotton candy machine! The concessions captain, Gary, entered through the back of the booth to deliver Kerry an update.

"Whelp, young lady, I've got some good news and some bad news. Which would you like to hear first?"

"Bad, I guess," Kerry replied exhaustedly, sitting slouched and wiping sweat from her brow.

Gary sighed, looking shamefully at the floor, "we're still trying to track down someone to fix the machine. I knew I should've taken that class! It's just … you know … life happened. The wife was …"

"Aaaaaaand the good news is?" interrupted Kerry.

"We're going to stay open until it's fixed. We aren't going to let a little a little hiccup like this stop the whole production!"

Kerry sat there, moist and defeated; her blood began to boil. The stupid fucking grin on Gary's face was genuine, which made it even more infuriating because Kerry saw nothing worth smiling about.

"The show must go on," he continued, "perseverance through the storm is what shapes who we become after we weather the storm!"

Gary obviously took his job very seriously. He continued to pontificate about how concessions were the nucleus of the entire fair, how 10 years ago he started "right here in this cotton candy booth" and within the next 10 years he'll be running the whole show. Gary continued on about how the life lessons she'll obtain in her booth will be much more valuable than a few extra hours of freedom will ever be.

Kerry was taught to always be reserved, and to refrain from having an opinion outside of what the Good Book says. Her outward demeanor may have been sweet and submissive, but her inner voice was very sarcastic and jaded. Few people shared her sense of humor back home, however she was the funniest person in her own brain, so in her own brain is where she preferred to be.

Going to college in a new city where nobody knew her was Kerry's opportunity to let her inner voice speak. Her first chance to do that was wearing a manila short-sleeved button-up and staring at her through coke bottle bifocals. Kerry stared back at the mini doughnut crumbs in the mahogany steel wool mustache covering Gary's upper lip, fantasizing about how good it would feel to punch him in it. She'd stopped listening to Gary talk at her and was ready to stop pretending to listen as well. Kerry's eye's grew large. She inhaled a deep breath and paused, poised as if she'd been frozen mid-sentence.

Nobody gives a shit, Gary! And neither should you! Not this much! It is the last day of an event that happen for a week once a year, and you're hanging your hat on a ten-year ascension up carnival mountain to become fucking Captain Cotton Candy!?! I mean, do you just sit around for the other fifty-one weeks waiting to matter? I know you're trying to impress whoever is in charge of this thing so you can fulfill your sad little carnie dreams, but c'mon dude—for what? There is no cotton candy in the cotton candy booth. Look around us, Gary, it's the last day, everything else is gone too! We have Mars Bars and Pepsi Free, which is a funny coincidence. Do you want to know how? Because Just like you, nobody likes them!

Kerry nearly spoke her thoughts in that moment. She felt sorry for him. Gary was clinging to a ridiculous dream because it was the only dream he had. Kerri just nodded, agreed and swallowed her frustrations.

Gary continued about his rounds and Kerry sat dismally, listening to the clock tick slowly. She leaned her elbows against the counter, head resting in her palms, and thought about how the first week of her new life was nothing like she dreamt it would be.

A large silhouette interrupted Kerry's wallowing gaze toward the summer sun. She assumed it was yet another cotton candy enthusiast she was going to have to disappoint. Just as she fixed her mouth to politely tell this mysterious fair-goer to fuck off, a gentleman drew close enough to see. What appeared to Kerry was a six-foot dreamboat in a neon yellow, mesh football jersey full of ambiguously brown skinned muscles. His name was Marty Christophers.

"May I have two cotton candy's please?" asked Marty, approaching the window.

"Huh?" she asked, both enamored and annoyed simultaneously.

"Two cotton candy!"

"Hungry?" she asked sarcastically.

Marty nonchalantly leaned on his elbow, shot Kerry a debonair stare, winked, and let her know that the second cotton candy would be for her. Kerry felt an oddly familiar, and powerful connection to Marty. A feeling she'd yet to share with anyone. When they locked eyes for the first time it felt as if their souls had known each other for a lifetime. After only speaking two words to him, Kerry felt she could say anything to Marty.

"Now what makes you believe that the cotton candy girl at the fair is just sitting around, waiting for some Adonis to not only come sweep her off her feet, but to do so, with the gift of something she's already thinly covered in front head to toe?"

Unphased and no less confident, Marty smiled and looked down for a moment.

"The only thing I heard you say just now is that you think I'm an Adonis."

Kerry reluctantly chuckled, "Well, you can't have any cotton candy even if I wanted some. The machine is broken."

"You could've led with that!" he said, shrugging with a vexed look on his face. "Maybe put up a sign or something? Why are you even here with no cotton candy?"

"You mean besides waiting patiently for Prince Charming to rescue me from cotton candy castle?" Kerry paused briefly to smirk. "I'm here because we have Mars Bars and Pepsi-Free!"

Kerry's resting face was very stoic. She spoke in a droll, sarcastic tone while pointing out her limited sundry like an apathetic Vanna White. Marty had not stopped smiling since he walked up to Kerry's booth. He became increasingly infatuated with every pithy word that came spilling out of her mouth. Most of the girls Marty talked to didn't have much to say back besides "totally" in between smacks of fruit stripe. Marty was entering senior year at NDSU as the quarterback and captain of the football team. He led the Thundering Herd to two conference championships in three consecutive title game appearances. Marty played basketball and ran track as well. However, not one of those activities put a tingle in his dingle.

Marty's father, a reverend at Lake Forest Baptist Church in Northern Illinois, envisioned his sons future by his side on the pulpit. Marty didn't have a distant vision of his life beyond one day having the freedom to do the opposite of his father's wishes. Football was a ticket out of his hometown and a free ride while he figured out where he wanted to go. Marty played basketball because Fargo was a hockey town, and the basketball team was terrible. His size, hue, and mediocre ball skills made Marty the go-to guy on a team where very few fans came to watch play, and which no one expected to win. Running track was a mandatory request from Marty's football coach to keep him in shape and out of trouble in the offseason.

Marty's true passion was in the theatre. Despite it being his field of study, Marty had little time to star in any school productions because of his athletic commitments. The closest he came to acting was modeling clothes for Woolworths in print ads and runway shows at the West Acre's Mall. Pretending to love his life in Levi's was no Shakespeare in the Park, but the money he made doing it kept the convertible he was restoring in his free time in pristine condition.

Marty was a walking, talking resume for a small-town Mr. Everything. He possessed the confidence, swagger, and smile of a young Billy Dee Williams and Burt Renolds combined. Marty was so quick with a joke it didn't matter if it was funny or not. He had an air about him that made you want to believe in him with an aloofness that made you want to believe he didn't realize it. He was a blast at parties and the apple of every girls eye on campus.

The sepia tones in his iris were beguiling to the doe eyed stares that got lost in his gaze. He liked talking to pretty girls, but most had little to say back. He appreciated how little effort it took to get laid, but afterwards, he'd lose interest faster than the flavor left the gum they were chewing.

"Pepsi Free is ridiculous," said Marty, with conviction, "It'll never last.

"What about Mars Bars?" she asked cheekily.

"What about them? I wasn't going to get into it, but Mars Bars are nothing but a janky Milky Way! Milky Way is horrible candy bar that never deserved to be replicated in the first place! You don't copy off the dumb kid in class!"

"Is that so?" asked Kerry. "I feel some hostility in your voice. Were you hurt by a Milky Way? Show me on this Mars Bar when the Milky Way touched you."

"Not so much hurt—definitely let down though. There's no balance; it's just too much nougat without crunch. At least Milky Way is consistent. Mars Bars are different in damn near every country you go to!"

"So, you've traveled the globe sampling exotic Mars Bars?" she asked.

"No, an old G.I. told me that once when I was young. All I know is that if I'm having a bad day in a worse place, I need a candy bar I can depend on to make me feel better. I can't be bothered with guessing games when the stakes are that high!"

"I don't understand how you can care so much about candy, or why a child would be hanging out with old war vets?"

"My daddy is a preacher," shrugged Marty, "he was always trying to fix wayward souls wherever we went. You meet some interesting cats along the way."

Kerry was pleasantly surprised by the coincidence. They shared a few moments of commiseration but forged a true connection while losing track of time through silly and nonsensical banter. Kerry's replacement was running late, and a line had started to form behind Marty. Neither seemed to notice.

The two of them could've stood there, ignoring the rest of the world together, all evening long. Kerry was finally relieved of her duties by Gary, who proudly martyred his sacrifice in place of the no-show evening crew.

The first thing Marty noticed as Kerry walked out of the booth was her firm—yet—ample farmgirl ass cheeks; spilling just slightly out the bottom of her Daisy Dukes. She trimmed the legs of her work jeans to just past the pockets. It was her first act as an independent, college woman.

Marty walked Kerry toward the security tent where here bicycle was parked. They held hands and meandered as slowly as possible without standing still to savor every moment of the short jaunt. Kerry's eyes were emerald and intoxicating, but hidden from the sun with her roommate's Esprit visor. Just a glimpse of them through a squint when Kerry looked up and smirked at Marty was enough to make him forget how to breathe.

They lingered a little while longer after arriving at Kerry's red Schwinn. They wore half smiles and shifted their gaze between each other's eyes and the ground around their feet.

"Thanks for walking me to my bicycle Marty …"

"These streets are dangerous out here," Marty smiled.

"I think the only thing that is dangerous around here is you, Mr. Christophers!" she said playfully.

"You have no idea, little girl."

"I'd like to find out." said Kerry.

Kerry fumbled with her bike lock while she waited for Marty to respond. The few seconds Marty took to hesitate, and chuckle felt like an eternity. Her mind raced.

Did that make me sound like a harlot? I'd like to find out… ha! Who do you think you are, Kerrigan Marie Panneli? Who does he think he is, taking so long to ask me out. At least ask for my number! Is he going to try and kiss me goodbye? I should make him work for it, but damn, if I don't want that man to jump my bones! I mean kiss me. I mean walk me home…Yeah, man, just stand there looking gorgeous, not saying anything. Ughh!

"So … I guess I'll see you around campus then?" Kerry asked.

"Well … we won today so we're partying at my place tonight," said Marty, "We could do that if you want?"

"You pre-planned a victory party? What if you lost?"

"Eh, some dance to remember, some dance to forget. A party is a party, right?"

"Well, when you sell it like that, how could a girl say no? Shall we go right now?"

"You don't want to go right now," Marty warned, "There is no one there but my roommates doing keg stands. Everyone will start showing up after 'Black Betty and the Ramble Lambs' play the Grandstand."

"A Ram Jam, cover band?" Kerry asked.

"Yeah. They're big here for some reason."

"Okay. That's perfect. It will give me time to shower off the sugar and regret from the last week of my life! What dorm do you live in?"

"I live in a house. Over on 12th street. I can pick you up and drive you there," Mary offered.

"Isn't that where all the frat houses are? Are you a frat boy, Marty?" Kerry asked with a distaste in her mouth.

"It's the football house. It's kind of rowdy at times but it beats bunk beds and an RA with a switch up his ass," said Marty.

"Must be nice to have that option, Mr. Football Star." said Kerry. "I don't just go riding around in cars with boys I don't know. I'm a pastor's daughter, after all." She smiled, winked and straddled her bike proudly like a southern debutant as she said this.

"I'm not just some boy. I'm the son of a preacher man." said Marty. "I know that being a pastors daughter didn't stop you from putting those shorts on this morning. Something tells me you'd like not to think so much about what your daddy says. Also, I'm going to pick you up in a pretty rad car. My Caddy took third in the car show earlier!"

"Wow, Billy Ray; third!" she replied facetiously. "Way to squeeze that little fun fact in the mix."

"Aren't you impressed?"

"Maybe if you'd taken first."

Kerry began to peddle off as she told Marty to pick her up at eight o'clock. He shouted back as she shrank into the horizon.

"Wait, how am I supposed to find you? I don't know where you live."

"It's a small campus, use your third place Cadilac to find me!"

Kerry blew Marty a kiss and waved goodbye, nearly crashing her bike as she tried to stay cool turning around.

II

Marty couldn't shake the moments he shared with Kerry, nor did he want to. Although his quest for love seemed impossible, Marty both welcomed, and rose to the challenge. On campus or at road games, Marty fucked with little effort. He didn't leave the house each morning with the intention to sleep with every girl he talked to, but he was open to the idea with most of them. Marty was about connections rather than conquest. He never premeditated a plan to swoon a girl before.

Marty picked up his buddy, Roger, for reinforcements. Roger Makowski was a shy calculus major that kept stats for the football team. He was present at every practice and every game, charting success percentages far more in-depth than anyone asked him to. Roger was practically invisible to the team unless he was getting picked on or standing at Marty's side. They became friends after Marty started sitting next to him at the front of the team bus to avoid the "Pre-Game Pussy Powwow" the rest of the team would have, bragging about all of the sex they weren't having.

Marty tossed his keys to roger as he approached the car. "I need you to take the wheel on this one buddy. You ready?" he asked, climbing up the trunk.

"You're trusting me to drive Jessabelle? I don't know, man. My dad's Ugo was already dented to shit when he gave it to me; a third-place Cadillac is too much pressure. Why are you climbing on the roof?"

"Because I don't know where this broad lives!" said Marty, "When we drive around looking, she has to be able to see me in case I don't see her first."

"That's crazy! No way!" Roger protested. "You're going to fall through the soft top if not completely off the side!"

"I've got great balance! Look, I can just straddle the sides like this. You just drive slowly and let me handle the rest."

"Can't we just let the top down? Stand on the seat if you must be so reckless."

Marty thought for a moment. "I'm already up here. You got this; I trust you, Rog. Just don't fuck it up." he said with a wink.

Roger drove Marty around campus slowly while he stood balancing on the roof of the Eldorado. They blasted the song *"Oh Sherrie,"* by Steve Perry, from the car speakers. Roger played and rewound the tape repeatedly, while Marty shouted to the music from the top of his lungs, changing the songs namesake from Sherrie to Kerry to bring it all home. An hour had passed before Kerry poked her head outside of her dorm room window.

"Marty?!" Kerry shouted, feeling both disgusted and flattered by the display she was witnessing.

The car was about a half of a block past her window before Marty figured out where his name was being called from. Quickly and carefully, Marty squatted down as far as he could to slap the windshield, signaling Roger to stop. Roger's mind hadn't been in the car since the third or fourth loop of the song. Startled, Roger slammed on the breaks, sending Marty rolling down the hood of the car until he hit the pavement. He lied there in defeat, sprawled out like a starfish.

Roger whipped the door open so quickly it bounces back and slammed on his legs. He ran to Marty's aid in hysteria to find him gently chuckling as he stared into the sky.

"Well, we found her, Rog," Marty said sarcastically.

"Marty I'm so sorry! Are you okay? Holy shit, if you're hurt and can't play, it'll be all my fault! I'm going to get pulverized! Please, please tell me that you're okay?!?"

"Yeah, Roger. I'm fine; relax! Now get lost."

"Are you sure?"

"Yes, I'm sure! I'll see you at the party!"

"Okay, Marty …" Roger said apprehensively, "you *are* still coming, right?

"Oh, I'll be coming tonight alright," said Marty giggling at his own wit, "I'll be at the party, too. It is my house, isn't it?"

"Yeah, well … are you guys gonna come right away? Or what time are you going to be back?"

"Just go to the party, Rog." Marty said with waning patience.

"Who's going to be there for me to hang out with until you get there?"

"Literally everyone we've known since freshman year! Nobody is going to tell you that you don't belong there, Roger! Scheider, Elk and Gasparini like you just fine. We hang out almost every day."

"The three stooges are *your* friends. They only put up with me because you do." argued Roger.

"I don't put up with you, Roger; you're my boy. I dig your rock collection, but most people don't want to hear about that shit; that's all. When you get there and see them, speak! Say hello when you walk into the room; don't just stand there and be awkward. Laugh when the others do. Look, Rog, nothing is out there to get you, but I'm not always going to be around to remind you of that. Ya dig?"

"Jeez! Okay, dad! I'll go to the party." Roger said, nodding his head.

He turned slowly to walk away, kicking pebbles down the pavement while he dragged his feet to Marty's house.

"Hey, Rog?" shouted Marty.

"Yeah, Marty?"

"Thanks, pal."

"Anything for you, buddy!" Roger grinned proudly.

Kerry approached the scene of the accident, trying her best to curtail laughter.

"You okay, Marty?" she asked with halfhearted seriousness. "Are you hurt?"

"A little," he admitted, "but it's mostly in my pride."

"Something tells me you may have some pride to spare; I think you'll be alright." Kerry giggled as she stroked Marty's face and helped him off the ground.

"Thank you," said Marty dusting himself off.

"This may sting a little bit though," Kerry paused, "You're a terrible singer! I mean, that was cute and all, but stick to football, kiddo!"

"Wow!" Marty shook his head. "Tough crowd! Are you always talking shit, or do you just enjoy giving me the business in particular?"

"I think it's just you, actually," Kerry shrugged. "I can't talk this way at home, so I guess I'm catching up for lost time. I feel oddly comfortable with ripping you apart, and you strangely seem to enjoy it for some reason, so why stop now?"

"Then don't. Just hop in the car and let's ride." Marty gestured towards the Cadilac. "I can be your tour guide and your punching bag!"

"Tour?" asked Kerry. "In your third place Cadilac? I thought we were going to a party?"

"What's the rush? The party isn't going anywhere. Allow me to squire a lady about town. Thou shalt witness all the cool shit."

Kerry rolled her eyes aggressively.

"What was that for?" asked Marty.

"That was at your Shakespeare … and for thinking that there is 'cool shit' in Fargo."

"The lady doth protest too much! Ye have little faith!"

"Oh gosh. Well, come what come may, I guess." Kerry tried her best not to smile as she pretended to be annoyed by his "Shakespearean" accent.

Marty stood with wide eyes and his head cocked in disbelief.

"What?" she asked. "Thou doth not have to be a theatre kid to know Shakespeare, stupid …"

"Fair enough. But most don't care unless thou art a child of the theatre."

"As good luck would have it … here I am."

"Let's go then," said Marty as he offered his arm to escort Kerry to the Eldorado. "We can ride for as little, or as long as you wish. Besides, you kind of owe me."

"Oh, do I now?" asked Kerry.

"Pretty much!"

"How do you figure?"

"Well, I did risk my life searching high and low to find you. I think that warrants a little one-on-one time," Marty said smirking and moving his hands like a tipping scale.

"That's a tad dramatic, but okay, Slick, I'm game. But first, will you answer one question for me?"

"Shoot," said Marty as he opened the passenger door.

"How many times have you done this whole 'car roof serenade' to get girls before?" she asked keeping eye contact with Marty as she sat down.

"Zero!" he assured her. "I saw it in *Teen Wolf*."

Marty shut Kerry's door and did a courtesy jog around the front of the car to get in on the driver side. He sat basking in the roar of his baby's V-8 as he turned the ignition key. Eyes closed, he could still feel Kerry staring at him, poised with a follow-up question.

"Hmmm … may I ask who you saw *Teen Wolf* with?

"No, you may not." Marty said abruptly. "You said you only had one question. Two questions is gonna cost you …"

"Just what, pray tell, is the cost of a second question, sir?"

Marty gripped the wheel with both hands, revved the engine and bobbed his eyebrows at Kerry.

"Dork! Let's go before I change my mind!"

▐▐▐

    Three hours of driving later, Kerry and Marty had seen almost nothing, yet shared almost everything about themselves. They wasted not one moment of their time together contemplating what to say next. They could speak freely to one another. The foreign concept of being listened to without judgement was a liberating experience. They could laugh and riff off one another in between much deeper, interpersonal connections--silky segues back and forth with jazzy, unrefined precision. The comedic chemistry between them was palpable. Even when they were bullshitting, none of it was bullshit.

    The only sight Marty took Kerry to see was the last stop of the evening. They pulled up to a lookout point in a town about a ten-minutes' drive away from campus--a popular destination for young adults and teenagers without privacy to get lucky. That night, the vista was empty because of the fair, which meant it belonged to the them.

    They lay together, under a blanket of constellations, on the hood of Marty's baby blue Eldorado; it was still lukewarm from the long drive. The crisp lake air, whispering secrets through the surrounding elm trees, balanced the heat radiating beneath them. Kerry rested her head on Marty's prodigious chest. The sound of his mellow, methodic heartbeat pulsated straight through Kerry's ear and into her soul. They shared heartbeats and a joint while they watched the moonlight bounce off the gentle ripples dancing across Lake Sakakawea in the distance.

    Kerry only hit the doobie once before letting Marty finish the job. She'd never smoked weed before; besides, she was already high on the aroma of neighboring lilac trees and the lingering scent of Drakkar Noir on Marty's hoody. The purple haze was just a bonus. They excused themselves to kiss the sky, reconvening in a world all their own--one so high, and far away from the others, it felt as if they'd never land again. It was the first time they'd shut up since they met each other.

They hadn't run out of words to speak; they just didn't need them anymore. The crickets courting each other, the owl preaching to the night sky, and the sound of silent, symbiotic synchronicity, was a sweeter soliloquy than either of them could have uttered to surmise such a sympatico. The tender stroke of Marty's strong yet curiously soft fingers through her wavy, auburn hair, said all that Kerry needed to hear.

Marty kissed Kerry gently on the crown of her head, breathing in the Finesse Shampoo, wafting from her freshly washed hair. Kerry titled her head back just slightly enough to make eye contact staring over her brow with innocently mischievous bedroom eyes. Kerry closed them slowly as Marty's lips drew closer to hers. Their first kiss was gentle only for an instant, then escalating rapidly to deep face French kissing, right before it graduated to passionate love making.

The heat radiating from their humping bodies was a beacon for an onslaught of eager mosquitos. They lay post-coitally with their sweaty backs fused to the hood of Marty's Cadillac, oblivious to the fact that they were being devoured. Those bloodsuckers may have had their way all night had it not been for that rustling sound near the bushes. The disturbance was just enough to startle Marty and snap the state of shared euphoria.

"Oh, shit! What was that?" asked Marty in a slight panic.

"What was what?" she asked.

"You didn't just hear that noise coming from over yonder?"

"Yonder? Who are you, Mark Twain?"

"I'll tell you who I'm not," said Marty matter of factly, "I'm not the Yankee about to check it out and get stabbed in the face by whatever's hiding in those bushes over there!"

Just then, a tiny red fox emerged from the brush. It scampered from it's hiding place until stopping ten feet in front of the car.

"It's just a little ol' baby fox," assured Kerry.

"Just a lil' ol' baby fox my ass. That mother fucker is a wild animal!"

"Fox don't eat people, you girl!" teased Kerry.

"I'm not trying to get bit, either!" Marty said defending himself. "You don't know what kind of day that fox had up to this moment. Look at him, sizing me up. He's got some frustration he needs to let out!"

They heard a faint bark growling louder in the distance.

"Did you hear that?" Marty asked frantically. "That sounded like a god damn wolf! Are you going to try and tell me that wolves don't eat people either?"

The fox sauntered off. Shortly thereafter, a feral labradoodle passed through their foreground chasing after the fox.

"Oh no! Look out for the big, bad, mangy puppy dog!" Kerry teased. "There wasn't much to do growing up besides watch the critters play. Nature is just a game, Marty. Those two were just passing through, playing tag, like they would have been if we weren't here. We may have given the pup a chance to catch up by distracting the fox for a couple seconds, but other than that, their game has nothing to do with us."

The expression on Marty's face was still uneasy and his body was rigid. It felt as if there was a hidden meaning in what she'd said, however, Marty's manhood would not allow him to admit there was no reason to be frightened.

"Marty, if you're still scared, why don't we just get in the car, close up the rag top, and lock the doors tightly?"

"I ain't scared of nothin'!" declared Marty. "But these mosquitos are eating my black ass alive, literally! Let's get back in the car."

"Okay, Marty." Kerry said, appeasing his masculinity.

They gathered their clothing and retreated inside the car. Marty turned on the car and spun the volume knob on the radio down to a nearly inaudible level. Kerry slid across the bench seat to claim space in Marty's aloof, yet tender embrace.

"I love that you said, 'rag top' by the way," said Marty.

She smiled and squeezed him a little tighter. "You've got your work cut out for you, Marty Christophers."

"Oh, do I?"

"Sure! If this is what a first date looks like with you, I can't even imagine what tomorrow will be like."

Marty hesitated. His face wore a wince of impending doom; he regrettably exhaled and replied, "Shit …"

"What do you mean, 'shit'?" she asked. "'Shit,' as in, 'shit, I already have plans for tomorrow, but the next day works'? Or 'shit' as in, a cocky way? Like, 'shit, girl, just wait and see!'?"

"I mean, 'shit' as in … oh I don't know how to make it sound clever. I'm dropping out of school and skipping town in the morning."

"You're what!? But why, Marty? Classes haven't even started yet."

"That seems like a perfect time to quit, doesn't it?"

"You are just going to drop a smoke bomb and leave without telling anyone?" asked Kerry. "What about me? I opened my heart, my soul and my flippin' legs to you, and you were just going to hit the open road without saying a word?"

"I'm sorry." Marty said. "I wasn't keeping it from you. I just haven't thought about tomorrow since I caught a hankering for some cotton candy. I swear I didn't plan it this way; I don't need to share my life story to get some. This just sort of happened. This wasn't your first time, was it?"

"Please. I've been to overnight church camp!" Kerry said defensively. She was lying, of course. She'd heard stories of lost 'V-cards' at Vacation Bible School but with her parents running the camps, Kerry couldn't wander far enough away to lose track of her virginity.

"Ha! That's crazy. I lost my virginity at a choir competition in Minneapolis!" Marty said reminiscing.

"Why should I believe you? You probably made up the party, just to blow it off and get me out in the woods to fool around, didn't you?"

"If I were lying to you all day, why would I stop now?"

Kerry thought for a moment. "Why'd you pick me up in your third-place Cadilac if you only lived a few blocks away?"

"Again, with the third-place business? You wouldn't tell me where you lived. Remember? You're the one who wanted to play hide and seek. Listen, the party is real, but truth be told, I never really wanted to go."

"But it's your house," said Kerry. "Why would you throw a party that you don't want to be a part of? Who are you now, the Great Gatsby?"

"Because if I went to the party, I'd have to lie all night. No one else knows I'm leaving and if they did, they would only try and make me stay. I need to get out of this fucking town, but they love it, and won't understand why I have to say goodbye. So, I'm not going to. I'm going to drive off into the sunset."

"Wouldn't you be driving off into the sunrise? You're a little too late for the sunset."

"Sunset was the plan before this welcomed detour." said Marty.

"What are you running away from, Marty? Is everyone loving you too hard to handle?"

He scoffed and shook his head. "Nobody loves me here. They love the feeling of winning football games; the name printed on the back of the jersey is irrelevant."

"When did you strike that epiphany?"

"A little bit after we won today. All the hands high-fiving me and patting me on the shoulder pads were attached to the same hicks that cursed my name and called for my expulsion after we lost the championship last year. I went undefeated for three seasons and won us two national championships. I make one mistake that happened to cost us a third title, then suddenly, 'I'm an affirmative action scholarship, and stealing opportunities from more deserving prospects!' It's bullshit!"

"Then just quit the football team," suggested Kerry, "stay here, finish school, and be my boyfriend. Maybe you can actually audition for a play, Mr. Shakespeare."

"I'll lose my scholarship if I don't play. It's kind of difficult to act in a school play if I'm not a student. There aren't many acting opportunities around here outside of the birthday clown at Hardee's. Believe me, that gig is not worth the free curly fries."

Marty continued to ramble on. He stared out the passenger-side window with existential longing. Kerry kept her gaze on him.

"To be honest," Marty continued, "I don't even like sports that much. Yeah, sure; I'm naturally gifted I guess, but the real gift was having an excuse not to spend my nights waiting for choir practice to be done or following my father around to whatever broken home or rec center he was trying to fix.

I got bigger, faster and stronger. Rec sports led to high school athletics, which led to a scholarship offer. I accepted the first opportunity to get out of my house, which is how we are sitting here talking to one another."

"I take it you aren't going back to Lake Forest, then?"

"For what?" he asked, whipping his head back to Kerry's attention. "So my dad can make me run a sports ministry for him in exchange for food and shelter? Fuck him! I'm tired of pretending to be who everyone wants me to be, so they'll love me. I'm going to Broadway to become a pro actor!"

"That seems like a logical solution!" Kerry said sarcastically. "But if all the world is a stage, and we are merely players, what is the point? Aren't you just exchanging one roll for another?"

"Maybe, but for the first time in my life I'll be in control of what role I'm playing. If they turned my life's story into a play, I'd barely be a bit player in my own production! I'm going to be a leading man in my life, as well as on the stage! This time, I'm going to create my own character arc. And I'll be damned if I'm going to live another day supporting someone else's storyline!"

"I get that, I guess," Kerry reluctantly admitted. "I put as many miles between me and my hometown as possible coming here. But what about our storyline? How serendipitous would it be if you met me right before you skipped town, then we fall in love and live happily ever after?"

"That would be sweet," Marty agreed, rubbing his chin. "and the way life ought to work, but what if it doesn't. What if I martyr my dreams in the name of love and we break up in two weeks? Our story arcs crossed one another today, and I'm grateful for that. Tonight, was amazing and unexpected; that's the coolest shit about it. If I stay, we've got to *be something* to make it worth it, that's not fair to either of us."

"This isn't some one-night fling to me; I think I might be in love with you!

"I, maybe, might be in love with you too … but neither one of us knows that for sure. I do know for sure that I can't stay here anymore. Who knows, Maybe the Big Apple won't be all that it's cracked up to be and I'll come running back to our serendipity. We can write each other just in case life really is like the movies."

Marty drove Kerry home, kissed her on the forehead and said goodbye. Kerry held back her tears and wished him well, then rushed out of the car and scurried up the walkway before Marty could see her cry. Marty sat parked outside of her dorm room window until he saw her lights turn on. Kerry looked out her window to see Marty's third-place Cadillac driving off into the sunrise.

I

Marty drove around town until he thought the party was over, planning to sneak in to get his stuff unnoticed. The hands of Marty's Swatch watch read 5 a.m. and the shindig was still in full affect. Luckily, everyone was so drunk they believed Marty when he told them he'd been there the whole night. He stuffed a Hefty bag with a pile of dirty clothes, a ticket stub from the fair, his third-place car show trophy, and a Folgers coffee can filled with the $582 he'd saved to start a new life, declaring he was taking out the trash. He walked out the door for the last time. The moment felt as if it were moving in slow motion, profound in Marty's mind; then Elk called Marty a gaylord for cleaning in the middle of a party.

The only thing Marty knew for sure about New York was that it was the place where his dreams were waiting for him. He wasn't even sure how to get there. Marty hopped on I-94 and drove toward Lake Forest as if he were headed home for the holidays and kept driving until the only thing in his rear-view mirror were corn fields and a setting sun. The risk of running into someone who knew his father was too great to stop anywhere in Illinois. Marty prayed Reverend Christophers had never been to the Turnpike Travel Plaza just outside of Cleveland.

After a good night's sleep and another whole day of driving, Marty made it to the Big Apple. It didn't take much time for him to realize that the now, $412 he had left to start his new life wasn't going to get him very far, living in a $100 per night hotel room. Marty drove up and down

Broadway, finally finding a space that he could call home until his big break came.

Weeks passed, audition after audition, without so much as a moment of stage time. The intense competition ranging from seasoned stage performers to newly trained Juilliard graduates hadn't entered into his calculations. Then, one afternoon, with his back pressed to the brick wall of the Palace Theatre and sulking after an unsuccessful attempt to audition *for Le' Misérables*, Marty was surprised by a voice.

"Chin up, Kermit!" the voice said with a chuckle. "I've been watching you out here! I know how hard you're working; you'll get your chance."

"Kermit?" Marty asked, lifting his eyes from the pavement to see a man dressed in acid washed jeans and a tight-fitting red leather jacket. The man stood with folded arms, shaking his head with a half-smile. "Sorry, dude. I think you've got the wrong guy. I'm new in town." Marty looked away, continuing to feel sorry for himself.

"Well, that's obvious!" said the man. "Sorry, that's just my humor. You'll get used to that. I called you Kermit because you're green. New to the game. You're all mopey like you aren't used to rejection yet. It ain't easy being green. Name's Travis. Travis Causgrove. Thespian, barista and proud gay man!"

"Oh. Okay. Marty Christophers," he said, extending his hand to shake Travis.' "I'm not gay, though; just so you know. Not a problem that you are. I just don't want you to get the wrong idea."

"Oh, thank you!" Travis said, sarcastically. "I'm sooo glad my lifestyle is okay with you, but you're not my type, Slick. Not to mention, your name makes you sound like a bumpkin. You're going to have to come up with something less hokey than Marty Christophers if you ever want to see your name on a marque. I've been where you seem to be before; that's all."

Travis heaved a theatrical sigh, "It would have been helpful if when I applied for my union card, they would have told me rejection is a part of the deal, but they didn't."

"What 'union' do you keep talking about? And what do you mean I'm not your type?"

"For one, I'm not into straight dudes anymore," said Travis. "I can easily tell that you're a raging hetero by your ability to somberly contemplate your life choices while simultaneously checking out every butt that passes your sight line. Secondly, I'm also very much in love with my partner, Terri, back in Queens. Third, but most importantly, what do you mean, 'what union am I talking about?' Did you really believe you could get a second of stage time without paying dues? Boy, this city is going to eat you alive!"

Marty laughed.

"Something funny?" asked Travis.

"Queens," Marty chuckled.

"Never heard that one before!" Travis said curtly. "Are you going to try your hand at stand-up comedy while you're at it? I hear The Cellar is looking for a nobody to headline Saturday night."

"I won't be a nobody for long, you'll see," declared Marty. "Where do I sign up for this union thing and how much does it cost? I only have a couple hundred bucks left to last me until I make it big. I'll buy you lunch if you take me there. Please?"

"Child," Travis said laughing, "Save your money, honey. I'm happy to help you however I can. I'm a sucker for lost souls trying to find their way."

"I insist! We aren't going to the Tavern on the Green. There is a Papaya Dog down the block next to my spot."

"You have a place on Broadway? No money, plans, or viable options to hold on to it, but you have a spot on Broadway?" asked Travis.

"Just off Broadway but close enough. What can I say? I got lucky, I guess. I know it won't last but we'll see what happens," said Marty.

The two of them walked down West 72nd Street toward Marty's car. Travis peppered him with pro tips to survive in the theater scene, as well as the big city as a whole. Travis had lived in New York his entire life. He and his mother moved from apartment to apartment throughout all five boroughs growing up while she struggled to make ends meet as a cabaret singer. Travis felt he knew everything there was to know about "the city that never sleeps." Marty felt as if he knew everything he needed to know about the entire world already, but appreciated Travis' confident kindness, so he listened politely until they reached Marty's Cadillac.

"Here she is, casa de la Christophers!" Marty said, presenting his vehicle/home. "Ain't she perdy?"

"On the outside, sure," Travis said, peeking into the back window. "But the inside is utter trash! Literally! No offense, of course."

"It's a little messy inside--I wasn't expecting company," Marty said through an awkward giggle.

"Company? When you said Papaya King was near your spot, I didn't imagine you meant a parking spot!" said Travis. "I thought you meant, like, you know, 'Hey brotha, come slide through my spot right fast.'"

Marty shrugged his shoulders. "Twenty-five cents an hour in the meter is the cheapest rent in town. Hector, the guy who owns this bodega, lets me use the toilet whenever I want!

All I have to do is buy a quarter-water or a candy bar. I don't trust most of the food; it looks pretty old. I'm good with footlongs and perogies anyways. What more could I ask for?"   "How about a roof that isn't made of cloth?" Travis chortled. "Oh, honey: Just wait until November."

"I thought I would be settled into something by now to be perfectly honest, but, hey… that's the life of a starving artist, right? Gotta pay those dues!" said Marty.

"You're going to be living the life of a frozen artist!" Travis said. "You can't live off street food, and Hector is probably planning to sell your kidneys. You're going to come stay with me and my Terri and I won't hear another word about it."

After a moment Marty gratefully accepted the offer. Shelter was nice, but having a return address to write on the cologne-stained envelopes that held the letters he'd been sending to Kerry back in Fargo was the best part of the deal. He'd taken great liberties in describing his success thus far, but Marty believed in himself so much that it didn't feel like lying.

His nest egg dwindled quickly. He sold Jessabelle to buy food, headshots and to chip in for his space on the couch in Travis and Terri's junior one-bedroom apartment. Once Marty's Cadillac money ran out, Travis got him a job figure modeling for art classes at NYU. Nude modeling was never in Marty's game plan, but it was the only paying gig he could land close enough to show business to put on a resume.

As time wore on, Marty's determination and faith in himself began to waver. Kerry still hadn't responded to any of his letters, and casting directors weren't responding to his unrefined acting chops. Despite his million-dollar smile and bravado, Marty was, deep down, just a scared midwestern boy, envisioning what life might have been like if he had stayed to just play football and be happy with the one who got away.

❚❚

Kerry wasn't managing the distance any better than Marty was, although for different reasons. Rumors began to flood the NDSU campus regarding Marty's whereabouts and the reasons for his sudden disappearance. Thanks to Roger's rendition of Kerry's account, the school and city surrounding it made her the scapegoat for the Thundering Herds sub-par season, and the harlot who drove away their superstar.

Ignoring dirty looks and blatant whispers took its toll on Kerry's mental health. She cared more about keeping up with her daytime soaps and what Victor was doing on *Days of Our Lives* than keeping up with her course load that semester. She wore the same dingy gray sweatpants and her roommate's old bleached-stained B.U.M. sweatshirt nearly every day to hide the weight she gained, and she avoided leaving her dorm room as often as possible.

The one class Kerry enjoyed and made some effort to attend was Psychology 101. Her professor Dr. Darlington scheduled a review day for the upcoming final exam that Kerry didn't want to miss. She fought through her exhaustion and queasy stomach to make it on time to her 8 a.m. class that frigid December morning. Kerry may not have been tardy to class that day, but she wasn't present either. She took a seat in the back row of the lecture hall, tucked her arms into her puffy, brown, ski jacket, laid her head to rest on the desk until class started, then fell sound asleep before the professor had the chance to say, "Good morning."

Dr. Darlington allowed Kerry to remain in her uninterrupted slumber until class was dismissed, and the lecture hall was empty. He sat, leaning back in his swivel chair with his feet propped on his cluttered desk and his hands clasped behind his head. He stared at Kerry above his glasses for ten minutes waiting for her to awaken naturally. Dr. Darlington eventually grew tired of this bit, and cleared his throat with obnoxious gusto as he sat down in the desk beside her,

"AH HEM!" Dr. Darlington coughed thunderously from the chair.

"Don't worry about who's baby it is!" Kerry exclaimed, in a half dream state.

"Who said anything about a baby, Ms. Panneli?" asked Dr. Darlington.

"Sorry about that, Mr. Darlington," she said in a daze. "I must have been dreaming."

"It's *Doctor* Darlington if you don't mind," he said. "I was actually a practitioner of psychiatry for several years before teaching the field of psychology. I apologize if my vast wealth of knowledge was putting you to sleep."

"Okay, sorry, *Dr.* Darlington." said Kerry with thinly veiled sarcasm. "I didn't mean to fall asleep. I'm, uhm, I'm just going through a lot right now. I'm trying my best, okay? At least I made it to class today. And I always call you when I'm too sick to make it."

"It's quite alright," said Dr. Darlington, "although I've told you repeatedly, you don't need to let me know when you are choosing not to come to my class. You aren't in high school anymore. I would however like to chat with you since I have you. Do you have a minute?"

"Do I have a choice?"

"You're an adult, young lady. You have a choice in whatever you want to do. You're the one paying to be here. You could've chosen to stay home and sleep. Instead, you chose to do it in my lecture hall. I get a paycheck whether you show up or not."

"Is this about my grades?"

"It was going to be, because I believe you are smarter than the effort you put forth, but I also believe that you know that already. I'd rather talk about that dream you were having."

"Oh, I see. Are you trying to 'Freud' me right now?" asked Kerry with an air of confrontation. "What do my dreams mean, Dr. D.?"

"I don't need to know how to interpret dreams to know morning sickness when I see it," he said. "I'm on my second wife and third child."

"Crap!" yelled Kerry. "Well, if you're planning on calling my parents, don't bother. They already know. I thought I could at least keep that a secret here on campus for a little longer. Am I really showing that much through my fat clothes?!? Just when I thought the rumor mill was slowing down. Well, you can spare me the lecture, doc; I'm sure it's the same one I get every time I call home. I know I fucked up!"

"Young lady, I don't need to lecture you about anything except personality disorders. Parent-teacher conferences aren't in my job description. For what it's worth, your belly isn't showing through your 'fat clothes' yet. Talks of you being pregnant with that Christophers boy's love child has been circulating since he went MIA."

"That doesn't make any sense!" shouted Kerry. "How could either one of us have possibly known that I was pregnant immediately after we made love? Are people around here so dumb they don't understand how the female body works?"

"Rumors don't have to make sense. The human brain needs a solution for every problem you introduce to it. If it's a problem we don't want to think too much about, we accept the first solution that comes our way. We pass it along without processing the information and move on with our lives, and on to the next problem to solve."

"No lectures, huh?

"You are just like my wife and daughter!" said Dr. Darlington. "You're too busy talking to listen. Look, I'm not a teacher, I'm just trying to re-retire sometime before I die. Most of the kids who walk through that door aren't going to do a darn thing with what I teach them after they walk out. If I can be of help to someone who actually needs it, then my time here is actually worth a damn."

"Why did you retire in the first place if you're so underappreciated?"

"You've obviously never been married." he said. "Home is the last place I would go to feel appreciated. Gwendoline is only 3 years old right now, but she has to go to college one day. I didn't factor having a child at 59 into my retirement plan. Nor did my wife, who's retirement plan was me."

"Gross!" she gagged.

"Excuse you?"

"I'm sorry. I didn't mean gross," Kerry back peddled. "It's just that you're so old! I was expecting your daughter to be an adult."

63 is the new 43, thank you very much." said Dr. Darlington with is chin in the air. "Darlington men have strong swimmers! A lot stronger than menopause, anyways. Lori was 47 when she got pregnant. I guess the woman in her family have strong uteruses as well."

"Well, I love discussing the vaginas of my professors' wives as much as the next gal, but I should probably go figure my life out," Kerry patted him on the hand. "Thanks for the pep talk."

"Okay then. Let's cut the bullshit!" said Dr. Darlington. "What are you going to do about the life inside of you?"

"Does it look like I have a fucking clue what I'm going to do about anything?" Kerry snapped. "My parents have already decided to give my unborn baby to a young barren couple from their church. They're interracial as well, so eventually no one else will know that it's adopted but me. I can't wait to watch someone else raise my kid every Sunday for the rest of my life."

She kept going.

"They won't even let me move back home or help me unless I participate in 'God's miracle brought forth in mysterious ways.' I can't stay here. I know I'm going to get expelled after my grades come out. But even if I don't, can you imagine what they'll say when it gets too warm to hide my shame with a puffy jacket? I already might as well have a giant scarlet *A* sewn on my Jansport!"

"You have while before that happens," assured Dr. Darlington. "What does the elusive Mr. Christophers have to say about all this? Do *you* know where he is?"

"Screw it! He's in New York!" Kerry confessed. "I was supposed to keep that a secret until he becomes a famous actor. He writes me letters telling me how close he is to breaking through the threshold of superstardom."

"Sounds like my son, Terrance," Dr. Darlington said, shaking his head. "He's out East as well, studying art history at NYU so he can find himself. The only thing he's breaking is my bank account. Well, that, and my heart a little bit each time he insists I call him Terri! Does Marty intend to grow up and come back to handle *his* responsibilities?"

"I'm sure he would be if he knew about them," Kerry sighed. "I can't bring myself to tell him, Doc. Well, at first, I couldn't because his letters didn't have a return address on them. By the time I could actually write back to him, I didn't know what to say anymore. I can't be the reason he doesn't make it. Don't you think that's the right thing to do?"

"Who knows what right is anymore?" he asked. "Was it right for Terrance to expect me to pay for his roommate and some vagrant they are allowing to squat on their couch to fly home with him for Thanksgiving?"

Kerry shrugged.

"Apparently it is! He can act like he isn't trying to punish me for refusing to call him Terri all he wants, but he refused to come home for Thanksgiving either way and Christmas isn't looking any better. According to my wife and her 3-year-old clone, his choices are my fault …" Dr. Darlington paused to stew, "and it's not even about the money; it's principle. It's not like his roommate doesn't come home with him every holiday as it is; I pay for that, don't I?"

Kerry fixed her mouth to speak to no avail.

"I mean, why can't he bring a nice girl home for a change?" his rant continued. "What's-his-name could still come. I'd happily buy three first-class tickets to Minnesota from anywhere in the world if one of them held the name of my future daughter-in-law."

"I'm sure Terrance will find love one day," interrupted Kerry, "but today, can we talk about me?"

"Sorry, I digress. I just wish my kids appreciated me more."

"You still have one left, Dr. D, cheer up. How old is your third kid?"

"Only two children bear the Darlington name," he stated matter of factly, "Gwendoline and Terrance."

"You said three earlier. Remember? Two wives and three pregnancies. I know you don't teach math but that equals three children."

"Oh, no, you misunderstood me. Allow me to elaborate. It's a bit of a long story."

"How long, Dr. D?" Kerry asked impatiently as the professor cleared his throat in preparation for a monologue.

"Oh, I'm sorry," he said bluntly. "do you have an appointment with a back-alley coat hanger to get to, or do you want my help?"

Dr. Darlington's crude and unexpected reference to abortion shocked Kerry into silence. She gestured him to continue.

"Thank you …" he paused for effect, "I met my first wife betty in college. Her friend Evelynn fell for my buddy Chuck and the four of us were inseparable until Betty left us a few years after Terrance was born."

"She left *you* with the baby?" she asked, slightly more interested in the story.

"Yes, ma'am," he said crossing his arms, "she said she felt called to be more than a Northwoods country bumpkin. It would have been nice of her to have said something before I built us our dream home in Lindinium. She could've said something before giving birth to a son she left me to raise alone. She could've said something while I was busting my ass after graduation. Double shifts in a greasy diner after a full case load during the day. I was a social worker at the time. *I* did all that for *our* dreams and it *still* wasn't enough."

"Where's Lindinium?" asked Kerry.

"It's about two and a half hours north of the Cities. So anyways, I pooled everything I had with Chuck's trust fund to buy the most beautiful plot of land. Five little acres next to a shallow lake on the edge of town. I could see our whole future there from the moment we stumbled upon it. Betty and I raising our family together in a house next door to Chuck and Evelynn with their kids. The giant Chestnut Oak in the middle of the property had 'treehouse' written all over it …"

"I'm sorry," she interrupted. "can I stop you for a minute? What cities are you two and a half hours away from? If I must listen to your whole life story, you can at least paint a clear picture for me."

"The Twin Cities, but my story could take place two and a half hours away from Timbuktu and it wouldn't make a difference. Please don't interrupt."

"Maybe I'll want to visit there some day. Twin Cities still means nothing to me."

Dr. Darlington sighed heavily through his nostrils, "Minneapolis and St. Paul? I know you aren't a geography major but certainly you've heard of at least one of those?"

Kerry thought for a moment, "Oh! That's why they call them the Minnesota Twins. Stupid. Anyways, that's super far away. You leave your wife and toddler all semester to teach freshman psych?"

"Just during the week," he said. I sleep in the R.V. that Lori and I were supposed to travel the country in after I retired. I go home on the weekends. A man does what he has to do to make ends meet. Now, where was I going with my story? We built the dream house; Betty left; Lynn gave birth to Maye … That's right. Evelynn was there for me after Betty left. Chuck sold shower curtain rings on the road, so he was always gone. He got a job in town after Lynnie told him she was expecting but he was still always working. I was there for her just like she was for me. So much so that it might as well have been my child she was carrying. That was the third pregnancy I was referring to."

Kerry stared discerningly. "Dr. D, were you and Evelynn, you know …"

"I don't." he said defensively. "You keep interrupting. Where was I?"

"Hopefully getting to a point. I kind of have to pee. I am pregnant, you know."

"Fine. The point is that life rarely works out the way you plan it. Evelynn died when Maye was 10. She's off to college now so chuck is shopping retirement villages in Boca. I started a successful psychiatry practice in the next town over and eventually fell in love with my secretary Lori. We had big retirement plans too, but guess what happened?"

"Your wife got pregnant with Gwendoline?"

"Then my wife had Gwendoline … six damn months into my retirement, my 47-year-old wife got pregnant. Biologically speaking, she should've been too old to conceive a child. But socially speaking, we were too old to consider any option but raising that child ourselves. Don't get me wrong; I love my daughter more than life itself! It's the one positive result of my marriage. I will never forget the moment I watched Gwendoline take her first breath. Nothing else mattered after her life became a reality."

"It's not that I don't want kids," said Kerry. "One day. I just finished being a kid, myself. It's not fair! I want my life to matter for a while!"

"It's not fair at all," agreed Dr. Darlington. "You can do everything right and by the book and still get screwed. What would be even more unjust is for a child to be raised by someone who wishes they didn't hold the responsibility. I think you'll make a fine mother when you are ready; but for now, I can help you find one who is."

⫼

Peter John Michael-Barry Panneli was born in the late evening of May 29, 1986. Kerry gave him the name of her father and uncles, a kiss on the forehead, then handed him over to the custody of the state. Kerry was certain whomever adopted her son would change his name, but they might keep one if she gave him enough of them. Until that day came, Pete was placed in the foster care of an elderly woman named Lonah Walker.

Lonah was a retired kindergarten teacher and closet poet from Northern California. She'd been widowed three times before having the chance to give birth to a child of her own. Her first husband Eldridge Walker died during the construction of the Golden Gate Bridge, just a few months shy of completion.

Lonah followed her second husband Lyle, a civil rights activist and member of the Black Panther Party, back to his hometown of Stone Mountain, Georgia. Lyle met his demise at the hands of the KKK. Lonah settle down with her third husband Stanley, a mild mannered and dependable accountant, in Fargo. Stanley died of pneumonia in 1972, which led Lonah to give up on romantic love, and began fostering children the following year.

Lonah was 70 years old when she took custody of Pete. She didn't have the energy to keep up with maladjusted pre-teens anymore, and felt an infant would be fine in the short term. Pete lived with Lonah until he was four years old. Over those four years, Pete and Lonah grew to be the best of friends.

Pete was an easygoing and imaginative child who was always content with his surroundings so long as he had his "Nonah." Lonah was an avid TV watcher, so together, they'd watch her favorite sitcoms on Nick at Nite before putting Pete to bed. They're daytime television lineup would consist of *The Today Show*, *The Price is Right*, and *Forever Young*, a soap opera about the intermingling love lives of doctors and patients in an amnesia ward; Lonah loved her stories.

Lonah also loved her junk food. She and Pete made daily visits to the corner store for Reese's Peanut Butter Cups, a small brown bag full of penny candy, and a can of ice-cold Pepsi they'd share while stopping to watch the older children play at the playground on their way home.

"Nonah?" asked Pete.

"Yes, Pookie?"

"Can I have a peanut butter cup?"

"I don't know, can you?" asked Lonah. Lonah might have been a sucker for an adorably mispronounced word here and there, but was a stickler when it came to proper grammar, even that of a 4-year-old.

"*May* I have a peanut butter cup? Pretty please!?" asked Pete, with prayer hands.

"I've only got two of them …"

"Perfect," said Pete, "one for me, and one for you."

"They give you two of them because they are tasty enough for one person to eat both of them. I let you choose your treat, and you asked the lady to make you a goodie bag. That's way better than one Reese's cup. You have all kinds of candy, Pete!"

"Here," said Pete sifting through his candy bag, "I'll give you four cherry balls for one cup."

Lonah looked down at Pete, sizing him up with playfully discerning eyes.

"Make it five, and you've got a deal … I guess."

"You drive a bargain, Nonah, but okay."

"You mean I drive a hard bargain, honey. And you better believe it. I've told you before; your Nonah is one tough cookie. I've been 'round the block a few times."

"I walk round the block with you every day, Nonah. Does that mean I'm a tough cookie too?"

"It sure does, baby," said Lonah with a giant smile, "and a cutie pie!"

Their midday ritual broke the monotony between the a.m. and p.m. television lineups. Pete and Lonah didn't venture many places beyond church and the grocery store. Lonah gathered all of her non-snack time grocery essentials every Thursday night with the *Grocery Getters*. It was a program the reverend of her church started in which he made the youth volunteer to help the elderly carry their groceries.

Lonah wasn't necessarily a religious person. She loved the energy that fueled the gospel music, extracting her own message and inspiration from the sermons. She thought it was safer to believe in something than nothing at all. "Too old to sin properly, anyways!" As she'd often think to herself. A couple hours once a week inside of a church to ensure a comfy space for all of eternity was the bargain of a lifetime in her mind.

Pete was too young for Sunday school, and there weren't enough kids his age to hold a daycare, so he sat with Lonah through service. Although, he couldn't sit for very long. Pete was usually under the pews, pretending to fix cars by pulling off the gum stuck to the bottoms by the halfway point in the church announcements. Once all of the cars were fixed, Pete enjoyed rolling underneath the pews and clipping the ankles of the unsuspecting participants in his game.

Some appreciated the comic relief amidst talks of eternal damnation and perpetual sacrifice. Others felt Pete lacked discipline and the rod had been spared on him too many times. They wore disgust for the toddlers blasphemy on their faces. Elder Caldwell, or God, according to Pete, would use that opportunity in his sermon to encourage the young adults to get married and start having children so the young Lamb of God, as he called Pete, would have someone to play with.

Reverend Caldwell's patience with Pete was due in large part to how sweet he was on Lonah. A widower himself, all of the woman older than 60 in the church were sweet on Elder Caldwell. One of those woman, Sister Bennet, resented Lonah for the reverend's repeated clemency on Pete's childish spasticity. Clarice Bennet was the wind and the water of the congregation's gossip mill; she made it her business to let everyone know how little business Lonah had raising a baby at her age.

"Bye-bye, Sister Walker. I'll be praying for you two!" shouted Sister Bennet from the front seat of the church van.

"Bless you, Clarice!" said Lonah through a forced smile. "Byyyyeee, Reverend Caldwell," she said looking past Clarice. "Thank you for the ride home! Pete, wave goodbye and say thank you to Reverend Caldwell."

"Oh, just doing the Lord's work, ma'am," said the reverend, modestly. "Pete, you take good care of Miss Walker now, you hear me? I'll see you two Thursday evening with the *Grocery Getters*."

"What does she need to pray for us for, Nonah?" Pete asked, grabbing Lonah's hand as they walked up the sidewalk.

"Nothing that is any of that old busybody's business, honey. Don't pay her any attention. Let's go inside; *Andy Griffith* is about to start."

"Can we go to the park, after?"

"Oh, I don't know, Petey Sweetie, Nonah is pretty tired," said Lonah, "How about we go tomorrow instead? You can move dirt around all morning!" she promised, referring to the toy excavator Pete enjoyed playing with in the sandbox.

"I want to ride the slide!"

"I definitely don't have the energy for that!" she said quickly.

"Good thing we aren't going until the morning then, huh, Nonah? You get energy again after you go to sleep. But, Nonah, what do you need so much energy for? All you have to do is sit and watch me."

"Not with all those hard-headed heathen older boys running around rough housing like they do. You could get trampled or fall off the slide. If I let something happen to you I don't what I would do!"

"But I am an older boy. I'm four now, Nonah; I can handle it."

"Oh, can you now?" she asked.

"Yup! You would be the only other Nonah out there. If all the other boys know how to slide alone, it can't be that hard."

"I'm the only Nonah anywhere, boy!"

"No. Like mommies," Pete corrected, "Nonah means the same thing."

"Nonah's are a lot like mommies," Lonah agreed, "Just a little older I guess."

"You're not my mommy, Nonah?" he asked with a big-eyed stare.

Oh, shit! Lonah thought to herself. Pete wore a look of puzzled devastation as he waited for an answer. Lonah had been dreading this moment since Pete could talk well enough to ask questions. She'd hoped the subject wouldn't come up until they found a set of parents to take Pete home.

"No, honey, I'm afraid I'm not. But I am your Nonah … and you're my little Pookie Dookie Petey! That's all that matters as far as I'm concerned!"

"Where is my mommy?"

"Your mommy is still growing up, sweetie," said Lonah. "After little children grow up, they become mommies and daddies, and make little children of their own. Sometimes, little children try to grow up too fast, and they have a baby before they're all done growing up. That's why your mommy and daddy gave you to me."

Pete grasped Lonah's hand tightly and stopped walking. He looked up at Lonah with fear and confusion in his tearful eyes. "My mommy didn't want me?"

"Of course, she did!" Lonah knelt down, holding Pete by the shoulders. "She wanted you to have the best life possible, but she knew she couldn't give that to you. A mommy and daddy's job is to love you, take care of you, and teach you how to be a grown-up one day; they can't do that if they are still children themselves."

"Will you teach me how to be a good grown-up since my mommy is still a little kid?"

"I'll do you one better, Pete. I'm going to allow you to be the best kid anyone has ever made! You're going to get a new mommy and daddy one day; we'll let them worry about all that grown-up stuff, okay? You have your whole life to be a grown-up; the only thing you need to worry about until then is staying a little boy for as long as you can!"

"How do I do that, Nonah?" he asked.

"By using your imagination, of course," she answered. "Today, let's pretend that we are in our favorite television programs, then tonight I will tell you your favorite story before we go night-night."

"Mr. Fat Man?" Pete asked, excitedly.

"Mr. Fat Man," confirmed Lonah.

"Mr. Fat Man"

"One day, there was a big ol' fat man walking down the street, as big as a house! He came across a little girl playing hopscotch on the sidewalk. He shouted, 'Hey, little girl!'"

Lonah was a very animated storyteller. When she spoke for the fat man, she spoke in a slow, deep voice, and wobbled side to side with bloated cheeks and flailing arms.

"'Move out of my way! I'm too fat to go around you!' The little girl looked up and said, 'Hey fat man, how'd you get so fat?' The fat man patted his belly and said, 'I ate a loaf a bread. I ate a dozen eggs. I drank a gallon of milk. I ate a stinky dog.' 'You ate a dog?' asked the little girl as she started running away. 'Yup! I swallowed it whole. I'll eat you, too, if I catch you!'"

The fat man catches the little girl and eats her. He continues to terrorize the neighborhood, listing everything he's eaten already before he devours another child. Pete's favorite part of the Fat Man Story was the finale. Lonah used Pete's name in the story and made him the hero. After Mr. Fat Man ate a dog, a little girl, a police officer, a firefighter, and a couple little boys and their football, he waddled up to Pete:

"'I'm too fast for you, fat man, you'll never catch me!! said Pete. 'That's what they all said before I ate them! Come here little boy!'"

"Does Pete get away?" Pete asked as if he didn't already know.

"Well, the fat man chased Pete, and Pete ran. And he ran. And he ran. Pete ran so fast, that he made the fat man trip and fall. The fat man landed on his belly, and it busted wide open; and out came the little girl.

Out came the stinky dog. Out came everyone that the fat man ate! All of the townspeople lifted little Pete on their shoulders and shouted, 'hurray!' The end."

"That was close!" said Pete, looking up from his little spoon position in Lonah's snuggle.

"Good thing you're so fast, boy!" said Lonah. "Roll over now; it's time to go night-night. Pleasant dreams; sweet dreams."

"Pleasant dreams; sweet dreams, Nonah."

Pete was rarely tired come bedtime. Ordinarily, he'd stare out the bedroom window and allow his mind to wander until his thoughts turned to dreams but tonight there was still a thought from the day he'd yet to make sense of.

"Nonah?"

"Yes, Pete?"

"Are you like *Isn't* Bee?"

"Am I like who?" asked Lonah, eyes closed, still laying on her back with hopes Pete's line of questioning will be brief.

"*Isn't* Bee! You know, from *Andy Griffin* … You always say that 'ain't' isn't a word."

"It's Aunt Bee, dear." she said with a chuckle. "They just have southern accents, but that is exceptionally good grammar, Pete."

"What's an accent?"

"It's what happens when too many folks stay in one space for too long." Lonah said, sitting up to attention. "Most of my second husbands family never left the house they grew up in! I couldn't understand a doggone thing any one of them would say to me, but they could understand each other perfectly!"

"So, are you like *Aunt* Bee, then?" asked Pete, rising up as Lonah did.

"In what way, honey?"

"Opie doesn't have a mom, but *Aunt* Bee takes care of him until Andy finds a wife and then she's his mom. That's like me and you, right?"

"I guess so, Pete."

"Well, it's almost like that," Pete said correcting himself. "Opie and *Aunt* Bee have their own rooms."

"Don't you like sharing a bed full of snuggles with me?" she asked, giving Pete a wiggly side-hug.

"Sure, Nonah, who doesn't?" he answered, embracing Lonah's love. "You can still come to my room and tell me stories before night-night, but when my mommy and daddy are done growing up, they will have a big house, so you'll probably have your own room."

Lonah walked around the bed and invited Pete to sit next to her on its edge.

"Oh, honey, I'm afraid I can't come with you after your new parents adopt you."

"You're not coming with me?" he asked, looking straight up at Lonah. But why?!? Aunt Bee will still lives with Opie and the Sheriff … why won't you come with me, Nonah?"

Pete's eye's began to well. He grasped Lonah's arm as a tear rolled down his cheek. She hugged him back with all of her strength and rocked him back and forth.

"Pete, I love you, so much! Do you know that?"

Pete wiped his tears on Lonah's housecoat and nodded slightly without lifting his head from her bosom.

"I will never, ever, ever stop loving you, no matter what!" she continued, squeezing Pete a little tighter. "Do you love Nonah, back?"

Pete looked up and nodded.

"Good! Then since you have a little piece of my heart, and I have a little piece of yours, I'll always be with you wherever you go. And you know what they say about folks that share hearts, don't you?"

Pete looked up and thought hard as if he might.

"I'll tell you what that means. That means one day, when your sitting in your own room, looking out a window like this one at night, I'll be able to feel it, and I'll come to my window. How about we make a plan to meet up at the stars every night-night?"

"Which one?" asked Pete. "There has to be a hundred stars up there."

"Point out the first star you see and that's where I'll meet you."

"Everyone picks the first star they look at. Too crowded. We need our own star!"

"Smart thinking, Pete," said Lonah. "You're absolutely right. How about the second star? To the right of the first one?"

"I like it, Nonah! A whole star all to ourselves … what will we do when we get there?"

"Anything you can imagine, Sweetie," Lonah promised. "All you need to do is get to that second star. Once you're there, you can do whatever you choose, and be whomever you like—anything you can dream up, straight on till morning."

"What happens in the morning?" asked Pete.

"We won't have to worry about that until the morning comes. We are both here together, right now and if we lay back down and think happy thoughts, we'll fly away towards that second star. I'll race you?"

"I'll be the winner, easy, Nonah." Pete said confidently. "Does it take a long time to get there? How high is the Second Star?"

"So high that it feels like you'll never land."

Lonah held Pete until she was sure he was fast asleep, then slowly and carefully inched her arm free. She crept back into the living room to watch *In the Heat of the Night* and tweak the prose of poem on which she'd been working. After Pete's night-night time was the only time Lonah had to be alone and create. On this night, however, Lonah's head hit the couch cushion before she had the chance to pick up her pen and notebook from the coffee table.

Pete woke up the next morning to find Lonah lying lifeless in the living room. He assumed she was still sleeping and must need more rest if she were so tired that she couldn't here Pete calling her name or feel him tugging on her arm. Pete went to the kitchen and helped himself to a bowl of Corn Pops and brought it back with him to the living room. It was the first time Pete made cereal on his own, but he'd been studying his Nonah's milk pouring technique for a while. He only spilled a little.

Pete was beginning to worry as Monday afternoon rolled around. Lonah had never slept that long before and she promised to take him to the park that day.

Ah, man! Nonah is going to have so much energy when she wakes up! She's been sleeping forever! Now we can stay and play at the park all day!

Pete repeated those thoughts as many times as he needed to until he believed them. He sat crossed legged on the floor in front of Lonah's dead body on the couch. His eyes stayed glued to the TV in a trance as if he were looking right through it. He got up occasionally to use the bathroom or rummage through the refrigerator for something easy to eat, but then right back to the television with a fresh sleeve of Ritz Crackers and a log of Braunschweiger that he bit from directly because he wasn't allowed to touch knives yet.

He brought blankets from the bedroom and made a pallet on the floor next to couch after the days programming had ended. He told Lonah the 'Mr. Fat Man' story and kissed her on the forehead.

"Pleasant dreams; sweet dreams, Nonah," Pete said just before lying down to stare at the ceiling until morning.

Episode Three ...

When Pete Met Gwendoline.

I

"Gwendoline, my darling little Darlington? What are you up to in here?" asked Dr. Darlington, knocking on his daughter's bedroom door as he walked in.

On the walls of Gwendoline's room hung a periodic table, a framed 8x10 photo of Albert Einstein sticking his tongue out, and two posters from the cartoon *Strawberry Shortcake*. It was the one television show Gwendoline's mother allowed her to watch each week. Blueberry Muffin was her favorite character, hanging just above the headboard of her bed, which matched the bed spread and window curtains. Huckleberry Pie was posted above her desk.

Gwendoline's desk was neat and meticulously organized to the placement of her protractor at a perfect 90-degree angle at the top right corner of her desk. With her globe, microscope and full set of *Encyclopedia Britannica* crowding her workspace, Gwendoline preferred to sprawl across the floor on her belly.

"Oh, you know, just doing summer math like the rest of the 8-year-olds in the world." replied Gwendoline without looking up.

Gwendoline was a highly intelligent child who excelled at everything she tried. Her parents recognized a potential for greatness early on and spread it thinly over multiple activities to protect said potential from being squandered. Piano lessons on Sunday evenings; equestrian and dressage every Monday and Wednesday; gymnastics on Tuesdays and

Thursdays; and summer soccer played on Saturdays with practice every day. Household chores and next year's homework was also a daily staple of Gwendoline's summer vacation itinerary.

"I didn't ask you to sass me, young lady."

"You also didn't ask a very smart question, Dad." said Gwendoline, gently slapping her pencil against her notebook. "You already knew what I was doing. You're the one making me do it, remember?"

"Well, summer homework is more of your mother's thing than mine, but …"

"Please, Dad!" she interrupted, looking up at him with a scowl. "Both of you are working together to steal my childhood."

"You wouldn't have a childhood without us," he exhaled and plopped onto Gwendoline's bed, "You should be grateful to have parents. We aren't trying to steal your childhood. It's our job to do everything we can to prepare you for adulthood. God willing, you're going to spend a lot more time in the latter. You might as well get ready for it before it sneaks up and bites you in the keister."

"How are times-tables supposed to get me ready to be a grown-up?"

"Because you'll never have to stop solving problems," Dr. Darlington said curtly, "Do you want to take a little break or are you going keep giving me a hard time?"

"You didn't say anything about a break …"

"You didn't let me; you were too busy acting like your mother!"

"Of course, I want a break!" Gwendoline emphatically shut her notebook. "Can I go paint something in mom's studio?"

"You know how she gets when you touch her art supplies," warned Dr. Darlington.

"Ugh!" said Gwendoline with an eye roll. "At least someone would be touching them. I bet you she wouldn't even notice …"

Gwendoline's mother, Lori, spent her life aspiring to be a famous painter—as soon as she found the time. She began several projects over the course of her adult life but had yet to finish a single one of them. She hadn't started a new painting since becoming pregnant with Gwendoline. She still loved her medium, but she was resentful of the "undeserved acclaim and admiration lesser artist were receiving for rushed and uninspired hotel art."

"That, my darling little Darlington is what you call a sucker bet. I wouldn't stake the last dollar of my worst enemy on your mother walking into her studio any time soon, but that is neither here nor there. What *is* here is a little boy who could really use a friend to play with."

"Is it Foster?" asked Gwendoline.

"Is it who?"

"I heard you and mom arguing about the Foster kid that was coming to live Jim and Maye next door … or is Foster his last name?"

"I've told you before; respect your elders. It's Mr. and Mrs. Hookston. I've also told you repeatedly to stop eavesdropping, you little busybody."

"Then you and mom shouldn't talk about what you don't want me to hear right in front of me! Mom said she wasn't raising another child she didn't ask for. You said, 'Not in front of Gwendoline,' which means you already knew I was listening. Then you said it would only be temporary. 'The kid has been through a lot' and you feel responsible, and this would be the safe way for Mr. and Mrs. Hookston to get a taste of what being parents is like. Then Mom said she doesn't understand why you care so much about that neighbor girl anyhow and …"

"Okay, Okay!" he surrendered. "I get it. I made a miniature stenographer. Maye's father and I have been best friends our entire lives; I know you've heard me say that before. I owe it to Chuck to look out for her like she was one of my own. He'd do the same for you. That is, if he weren't off in Boca Raton enjoying his retirement."

Dr. Darlington's gaze traveled out the window with a jealous grimace on his face, thinking about the life he planned that didn't come to fruition.

"Tortoise and hair my foot!" he said without context.

"What are you talking about now, Dad?"

"Nothing …" he said morosely. "Will you please just go play with the kid? Everything is an ordeal with you. That poor boy sat next to his dead caretaker like a sad Golden Retriever for four days before someone from the lady's church found them. He hasn't complained once since I picked him up. He hasn't really said anything now that I think about it … but not complaining is something you could try a little more. Look out your window; he's just sitting there, alone, in your brother's treehouse. He needs a friend."

"Gwendoline pressed herself up from the floor reluctantly. "Four days?" she asked, walking towards the window. "How did he eat? What did he do with all that time by himself?"

Gwendoline imagined what it would feel like to be unbothered for a week and became envious.

"For God's sake, don't ask him that! Or anything about what happened. Only happy thoughts, okay?"

❚❚

Phillip Archibald Darlington Jr. and Charles Thaddeus Hookston grew up together in Hibbing, Minnesota. Chuck was the son of mining tycoon, Thaddeus Hookston. Dr. Darlington's father, Phillip Sr., was a miner for Hookston Mining Company. Neither Chuck nor Phil wished to follow in each of their father's footsteps, so they left the Iron Range to attend school at the University of Minnesota in 1940. Phillip Jr. on an academic scholarship and with what he'd saved over the years shoveling snow, raking leaves, cutting grass and pumping gas at the Amoco station in Chisolm. Chuck's ride to higher education was funded by family money under the assumption he'd apply his degree to the family business.

They found themselves a couple of girls to date around halfway through the first semester. Chuck sat next to Evelynn Manderfeld, a pretty brunette from Copper Harbor, Michigan, in econ class; Phillip Jr. occupied her roommate, Betty Albertson, on double dates. Betty grew up in Edina, a wealthy suburb of Minneapolis. The four of them were inseparable. From as many classes together as possible and part-time jobs at the Gopher Hole Pop Shop, on through to graduation and the joint wedding and honeymoon they shared together.

They loaded themselves and a modest amount of camping equipment into Phillip Jr.'s Hudson and drove north up old US 61. Their final destination was supposed to be in the small harbor town of Grand Marais and then into the Boundary Waters Canoe Area. The eastern hub of the BWCA was in Ely, which is where the boys grew up entering the wilderness reserve on fishing trips, but they wanted to share a piece of their childhood with their new wives without having to honeymoon so close to their hometown.

The drive would have taken around four hours had they not pulled over halfway so chuck could use the bathroom. He peed near an overgrown trailhead that cut through a dense forest of red pines. The foursome followed the trail for a half mile and stumbled upon a small clearing at the mouth of a tiny lake. They decided to camp there for the night. The guys fetched the tents and set them up facing the water on opposite sides of a lone-standing, giant chestnut oak tree. The water was waist deep, murky and full of lily pads. Not an enticing swimming hole, but it was the perfect backdrop to stare at the future in front of them.

The small clearing was at the ass end of a five-acre plot of wilderness that happened to be for sale. It sat at the edge of the Lindinium city limits and bordered the neighboring Native American reservation town, Gawikaki. At thirty dollars an acre, the opportunity was too fateful to let pass them by. Chuck emptied his trust fund to build him and Evelynn a modest split-level with a den, master bedroom, and spare room for house guests or a child one day.

Phillip Jr. and Betty rented a small apartment near campus in Dinkytown. They both worked full-time at the Gopher Hole Diner while they saved up to build their dream home and Phillip Jr. pursued his master's degree in social work and doctorate in psychiatry. His vision for their home was too perfect to rush. He saw a two-story colonial with four bedrooms so all three of their projected children could have their own room. His den was to be twice the size of Chuck's with bookshelves covering the walls from floor to ceiling.

It took some time, but Dr. Darlington and Betty settled into their woodland oasis in Lindinium with all the desired specs met. The doctor began making family plans with Betty and drawing up plans for a shared garage with Chuck. There were also preliminary plans for the treehouse they'd construct with their eventual sons. Betty was the first to give birth, to their son, Terrance, in 1960. Although not for lack of trying, Evelynn didn't follow suit until '68 when she gave birth to a girl, Maye.

Maye was the spitting image of her mother and even grew up to follow in her footsteps-- not only by attending her alma mater, but also by falling in love with the man she'd eventually marry there. His name was Jim Jorgenson. A guitar-playing slacker from Lindstrom who loved fishing, smoking weed and, from the moment he saw her, Maye Hookston. Maye had been fantasizing about her dream wedding and having a family of her own since she turned 11, just after her mother died of Leukemia.

Jim Never thought much about the future. He had high hopes for his folk-funk cover band Little Fish Town to make it big but until then, his weekend and summer job back home at Bobber's Bait & Tackle paid him enough to take Maye on cheeseburger dates and keep his dugout full of stinky weed; that was good enough for the moment. That moment passed quickly into graduation day. Maye earned her business administration degree and was eager to start the life with Jim she'd been planning for years. None of Maye's plans had anything to do with what's she'd do with her diploma after graduation, and everything to do with saying, "I do" as soon as possible after graduation. Jim fell short of walking away with his communications degree, but he popped the question and followed Maye back to Lindinium just the same.

Maye wished her mother could have been alive to see her walk down the aisle, but beyond that, she and Jim had the backyard wedding Maye always dreamed about: Her five best gal friends in pink chiffon bridesmaids dresses; a home-crafted gazebo near the shoreline; and everyone watching her march towards it in an elegant gown with an obnoxiously long train. She didn't picture so many of her father's sales buddies from over the years to be in attendance, but Maye didn't mind. The reception doubled as a retirement party for Chuck and all of his friends gave them cash in envelopes with a hole to see the face on the twenty-dollar bill as wedding presents.

Jim moved into the house where Maye grew up. Chuck gifted the dwelling to the newlyweds as a graduation present to Maye on his way to Boca. Jim dropped out and got a job unloading ships for the Lake Superior Grain Silos while he looked for something better. The hours were early morning, but as unmotivated as Jim was towards most things in his life, getting up at dawn was not one of them thanks to his love of angling.

The work was repetitive heavy lifting but the eye-level view of a sunrise breaching the horizon line of Lake Superior never got old. Although far more breathtaking on this freshwater ocean, the view reminded Jim of the mornings he spent in the middle of Lake Lynn, back home. Jim lived a short jaunt from the lake through sparce woods. He'd portage and paddle the family canoe out to wake and bake under the guise of fishing every morning before school.

Jim hoped to stash some cash away and get some momentum rolling with his music before he and Maye started making babies. Maye didn't want to wait however long it might have taken Jim to feel financially stable. Dr. Darlington was still assigned to Pete's case and was responsible for finding him a home outside of the orphanage he'd been living in since Lonah's death. Pete coming to live with Jim and Maye was the closest thing to a middle ground they produced.

Pete spent the first few hours at his new home in the treehouse outside of it. Maye looked out on him from her living room window. There wasn't much to be seen inside the treehouse from such a low angle; however, every once in a while, Maye would catch a glimpse of Pete's head bobbing spastically past the window cutout.

"He's been up there for a long time, Jim. What do you think he's doing up there? Shouldn't we go get him or something?" Maye asked.

Jim sat on the couch, strumming his guitar while he listened to the Twins play baseball on the radio. "Don't ask me. The kid came in talking about wolfmen and shit. I know he's been through a lot and all, but I don't think he knows the difference between reality and his imagination."

"What four-year-old does, Jim? It doesn't mean he's damaged. He's just being a normal kid."

"I don't see how any kid could sit and watch T.V. next to a corpse for four days and be normal afterwards. I don't know how to deal with that! Do you?"

"We'll figure it out. You just have to go with it." she assured him.

"It seems like all I do is go with it, honey," Jim said, standing up for himself timidly.

"What's that supposed to mean, dear?" Maye asked as she turned around with her arms folded across her chest.

"Nothing. It's just that, well," Jim rubbed the back of his head, trying to find the right words. "You know that I love you more than anything in this world. I would do anything to make you happy. I even took your last name when we got married!"

Maye walked to the couch and sat next to Jim, grasping his arm tenderly. "And I love you so much for that, James! It takes a real man to go to the lengths you do to make me smile."

"Tell that to my father!"

Jim and his father, Franklin Jorgenson, hadn't been on speaking terms since the minister pronounced Jim and Maye, Mr. and Mrs. Hookston at the wedding. Frank was already angry with Jim for dropping out of school before the surprise ending to the Jorgenson family line. He worked double shifts and weekends, both at the August Schell's Brewing Company and Pillsbury Flour Mill to send his son to college and give him a better life than the one he had.

"See there? Don't you want to be everything your father wasn't? This is your chance-- with a boy who desperately needs a father figure!"

"I know that. And I do, someday! The old-fashioned way, though. Like, handing out cigars to my buddies in the waiting room after you gave birth to *my* baby boy. I just think we are moving too fast. I mean, I haven't had the time to cast a line all summer."

"You have a lake right there in our backyard, honey. You can teach Pete how to fish. How about that?"

"No. I had a lake in my backyard back in Lindstrom. I'd be lucky to catch bait in that pond out there," he said, pointing towards the backyard. "It's not just that though. I miss so much rehearsal I'm afraid I'm going to get kicked out of my own band! We have something planned with your friends that is too important for us to miss every weekend. Did I tell you they changed our name to The Rounded Anglers last weekend while we were at your friend Joanne's baby shower?"

"You tell me about a name change every other month," she said. "How is anyone ever going to know who you are if you keep changing the name of your band?"

"You won't be questioning our process when we are selling out arenas like Guns N' Roses. I swear, we are just one song away."

"From what, Jim? Having a song? You guys don't even play your own music."

"Maybe we would if I had more time to write songs."

"Our life isn't in Lindstrom, Jim. It's here. Do you think we could afford a home like this one, the one my father gave us, with you working for Bob in the bait shop for the rest of our lives? We are only going to have Pete for a little while anyhow. I promise to give you some time to play with your friends before we have a child of our own, okay? Look out the window. Little Gwendoline is climbing up the tree to play with him. We have a built-in babysitter! I told you being parents was going to be easy. Our life is good, baby. Just go with it."

Gwendoline poked her head up through the opening in the treehouse floor to find Pete, punching and kicking at the air. He didn't realize Gwendoline was watching until an imaginary flying kick to his chest sent him stumbling in her direction. He paused for only an instant before delivering a swift spin kick high above Gwendoline's head.

"Was that kick aimed at me?" Gwendoline asked with a pang of offense as she hoisted her lower half into the treehouse.

Pete finished off an elaborate kick-punch combo, rested his hands on his knees while he caught his breath, and looked at Gwendoline as he stood up straight.

"There was, 'Foot' next to you," he said.

"I know. It was *your* foot, and it was way too close to my face!" she said.

"No, The Foot Clan! They were going to get you; I beat them up just in time, though, so don't worry."

Gwendoline wasn't well versed in The Ninja Turtles, and her over-scheduled young life didn't leave much free space for daydreaming. Imagination wasn't one of Gwendoline's many natural gifts, however, with Pete, she did her best to logic her way through it.

"What's a foot clan?" asked Gwendoline.

"The evil ninjas lying dead on the floor. Don't you see them by your feet?" he asked as if it were obvious.

"Oh boy, well thank you for saving me then," she said, playing along.

"You're welcome, girl," he said with folded arms and the proud look of a hero on his face. "The Shredder sent The Foot after me, not you."

"Why is The Shredder after you?" she asked, almost sincerely.

"He's the bad guy, and I fight crime" he said, shrugging. "That's just what we do. He must have found out that I'm out here all alone."

"Why are you out here all alone?"

"Because the rest of the turtles don't get me!" he said defensively. "They think I'm weird, but I don't need them; I can beat The Shredder by myself! Why do you ask so many questions, girl?

"My name isn't girl," said Gwendoline.

"Then why did you call me boy? Pick a game and stick to it. My real name is Pete."

"I think you mean you're real name is Peter," corrected Gwendoline, "Pete is short for Peter."

"No. Pete is long for Pete."

"Whatever you say, kid … but I like Peter better."

"What's your name, kid?" asked Pete.

"Gwendoline," she said proudly.

Pete thought to himself for a moment. *What's short for that? Gwen-da-line …ha … Gwenda-land sounds like a carnival. Gwendy-land would sounds more fun … Wendy's-land would be a hamburger carnival …*

"Is that long for Wendy?" he asked.

"Wendy?" she answered sourly. "Ick! That's not my name. Do I look like a hamburger princess to you?"

"You would if you went as her for Halloween … but I like Wendy, though," Pete said shrugging his shoulders as if the matter was settled and continued flailing pseudo karate moves around the treehouse.

"Now what are you doing?" asked Gwendoline, trying her best to keep up with Pete's imagination.

"Can't you see?" he asked as if it were obvious. "The Foot Clan is coming back to life!"

"I'll help you," she offered, "I can be a turtle."

Pete stared blankly at Gwendoline. "You can't be a turtle."

"Why not?"

"Because you're a girl; the turtles are boys!"

"Girls can be turtles too!" exclaimed Gwendoline with angry fists at her hips.

"Not ninja turtles!" he rebutted.

"I can be whatever I want to be-- even though my mother always tells me I'm going to be a lawyer because I like to argue so much!"

"We aren't playing Perry Mason right now," he said, "it's Teenage Mutant Ninja Turtles! You can be April O'Neil if you want?" he continued, offering consolation.

"Is she a turtle?"

"No, she is a reporter, but she's a friend to me and my brothers. We save her life sometimes.

"I want to fight too! April is a ninja reporter now. What do you think about that?" she said combatively.

"April doesn't know karate, but I guess I can teach you some moves really quick," he said. "Just don't tell Master Splinter."

"My lips are sealed." Gwendoline pretended to zip her mouth shut, lock it up and then throw away the key. The two of them climbed out of the treehouse to commence ninja training. Pete paused a few steps from the tree. His eyes glistened from tears fighting to stay in their ducts and he wore a grin just slightly enough to see the bottoms of his two front teeth.

"What's the matter, Peter?" asked Gwendoline upon discovering Pete was no longer by her side.

"It's Raphael. You gotta call me by my turtle name."

"Fine," she said reluctantly. "What's the matter, Raphael?

"You're weird too, huh?"

"Are you calling me weird, or are you asking me if I'm aware that I'm weird?"

"I don't know. The other kids at the orpans' edge said I'm weird, and you do the same stuff I do, so you must be weird too."

"Well, I don't think I'm weird, and I don't think you are either," she said. "Those kids at the *orphanage* who told you that are buttheads!"

"I bet they fart out of their nose!" Pete said with a belly laugh, thinking about the image of butt cheeks where a head should be.

III

Pete occupied every time slot Gwendoline had available that summer. He struggled to figure out what role Maye and Jim were supposed to play in his life, but Gwendoline was always a friend to play with. He didn't have to think much about that. Gwendoline had fun playing with Pete but what she appreciated most was a break from her responsibilities.

They pretended to be Ninja Turtles, Ghostbusters and any other cartoon character Pete was infatuated with on a given day. The two of them picked dandelions, held the stems and popped the flowers off; chased lightning bugs at dusk; and went on treasure hunts to find skippers to throw across the lake. Pete cheered her on during her soccer games, waited patiently for her piano lessons to end, and tagged along to anywhere Lori would allow him. There was little that could separate the two of them from each other's hips until September neared.

Gwendoline was starting the third grade, and it was time to go back-to-school shopping. She enjoyed picking out the best supplies to help her get the best grades, and she looked forward to choosing new clothes to show her classmates how much she'd changed and matured over the summer. Lori and Gwendoline had made supply shopping into a special event that the two of them shared since she began kindergarten. They would have lunch in between supplies and clothes, then see a movie at the Cinema 8 after they'd finished shopping. Gwendoline got to pick where they ate lunch and what movie they saw. It was the one day out of the year Gwendoline felt in control of her choices.

Pete was more excited to go school-shopping than Gwendoline. To his dismay, he was not invited to attend the mother-daughter tradition. He watched the two of them pull down the half mile gravel driveway, then huffed and puffed his way back inside his house.

"Why the long face, kiddo?" asked Maye from behind the *Cosmopolitan* she was reading at the dining room table.

"Wendy left me!" Pete said, pouting from the doorway.

"Aww. My poor baby! Come tell me all about it!" said Maye, patting her thighs, inviting him to sit on her lap.

"It's not fair! I want to play school too!" Pete complained as he hoisted himself into Maye's embrace.

"You want to play school?" she asked with a playfully disgusted expression on her face.
"That doesn't sound like a very fun game, silly!"

"Wendy thinks it is. She's been talking about it all summer, but she went without me!"

"She only went school shopping, honey! Her mommy took her to get supplies before school starts, but she'll be back later."

"What about my supplies? I can't start school without supplies! What are supplies, again?" whined Pete.

"You're not starting school yet, Pete. You have a whole year before you need pencils and Trapper Keepers of your own. Gwendoline is a little older than you, so she has to go to school every day, but you still get to stay home and play all day! Isn't that wonderful?!?"

"Who am I going to play with while Wendy is at school?" he asked.

"What about me?" she asked, leaning dramatically to the side to look Pete in the eyes, grasping her chest in jovial disbelief.

"You're too grown up to play games."

"Just because I'm a grown-up doesn't mean we can't have fun!" she said.

"Okay!" Pete said gleefully. "Do you want to go play in the treehouse?"

"I'm afraid I have, unfortunately, grown up too big to fit in that treehouse. I haven't climbed that thing since I was a little girl! How about something on the ground?" Maye suggested.

"How about 'Doctor'?" asked Pete.

"Excuse me?!?! Play what? Where did you learn that game?" she asked with frantic concern.

"From the stories. I want to be a doctor when I grow up, like Vance Dexter!"

"Vance Dexter? From that soap opera *Forever Young*?" she asked with slight relief.

"Yup! This is the *amnoosha* ward, and we help people *member* stuff. Okay?"

"You're too much, Pete!" Maye said, trying her best not to laugh. "You know what? Now that I think about it, you kind of do look like Dr. Dexter. Yeah. In the nose. Maybe you *will* be a doctor one day!"

"Do you really think so?" he asked with hope in his eyes.

"Sure! Why not?" she shrugged. "If you grow up to be as handsome as Christophe Martin, you can be whatever you want to be … one day. Today, let's focus on some kid stories. How about that?"

"I like stories. Nonah told me stories all the time! Do you know the one about the fat man?"

"I can't say that I do. I'm out of touch with the new stuff. I was much more of a book worm when I was little. Do you like to read books, Pete?"

Pete shrugged his shoulders. "I don't know how to read yet."

Maye shook her head and smirked. "Of course not. I forget sometimes that you're just a baby."

"I'm not a baby! I'm almost four and a half! I know some words …" he said with waning confidence. "Are big kids 'posed to read?"

"Everyone reads! Even grown-ups when they have the time!" Maye swayed from left to right in whimsical reminiscence. "Oh, my goodness, honey. Books were the best! You can go anywhere in the world or space through words and pictures! Let me think. I gave all my childhood books to Gwendoline when she was born and, if I remember correctly, Uncle Phil stashed them somewhere when Gwendoline outgrew them. Those books are a valuable treasure, no doubt about it. It might be hard to find, though. We are going to have to hunt a little bit. Are you up for a treasure hunt, Pete?"

"You know I'm up for a treasure hunt! I'm really good at them! You can even ask Wendy! Who is Uncle Phil, though?"

"Oh, that's just what I call Dr. Darlington next door because he was like a second father to me growing up!"

Two dads? Pete thought to himself enviously.

The two of them went to the Darlington house and scoured through the junk tucked away in the extra room at the end of the hallway until finding a box marked "MISC. BOOKS." Anything not deemed worthy of gracing space on the floor-to-ceiling bookshelf in Dr. Darlington's den was thrown in a box for the rummage sale they planned to have one day.

"What about this one?" Pete asked, holding up one of Lori's old Harlequin Romance novels.

"Hmm … too thick," said Maye, thinking quickly. "Keep digging. Thin-to-win, Pete. The short books are way more fun!"

Pete sifted through the pile of books and found two that he wanted to take with him: *Puppies are Like That* and *Cookie Monster and The Cookie Tree.* Maye read each book to him twice, at Pete's request. By the end of story time, Pete had forgotten all about being abandoned by Gwendoline and was back to running around the house by himself, blasting ghosts with his imaginary proton pack.

Jim came home from work that evening to shots fired as he walked through the front door. They came from Pete and his broomstick gun. Jim was exhausted and not in a mood to pretend.

"Hey there, Pete. It's nice to see you too!" Jim said sarcastically. "How is Gwendoline surviving without her little shadow?"

"You can't take your shadow off," Pete stated bluntly. "She took it with her to school shopping."

"Oh, I see. My mistake," Jim said.

"Hurry, Ray! Shut the door before the Wolfman gets in behind you!"

"What?" Jim asked with waning patience in his voice.

"You know, honey … the wolf man!" Maye interjected, signaling Jim to play along.

"I don't ever know what he's talking about. Who the hell is Ray?"

"Relax, Jim." said Maye. "I don't always know either, but it's obviously a game he's playing. Haven't you ever played a game?"

"Baseball! Now that's a game! If he were a little fonder of *that* game, we might have something to talk about!" Jim kicked off his shoes, adjourned to his spot on the couch, and tuned the radio to AM 610 in an attempt to tune out Pete's silliness.

"You *just* got into baseball, Jim," said Maye. "Out of the apparent thin air, I might add! You don't even know enough to talk about it."

"I know the Twins are in a pennant race right now!"

"What does that even mean? They win a little flag?"

"I don't have time to explain it to you; the game is about to go into extra innings on the radio. I was hoping to relax and finish listening to it after a long grueling day at work."

"Ugh, it's even more stupid that you listen to it on the radio!" Maye said. "What a boring hobby!"

"Well, it's about the last one I have," said Jim. "I haven't made it to a rehearsal all summer. I've got a lake in my backyard with no boat to fish out of, I can't even smo … uhm … swim! I can't even swim."

A set of headlights shined through the window, redirecting Maye's Are-you-serious? stare away from Jim and out the living room window. Lori and Gwendoline were coming home from their day of shopping.

"Pete? I think I hear Gwendoline coming home," said Maye. "Why don't you run over and see all the cool stuff she picked out?"

Pete didn't hesitate; nor did Maye waste any time picking up the impending argument from where she and Jim left it.

"Will you not talk about *marijuana* in front of him like that?" Maye said softly, as if Pete could hear her from outside. "I'm sorry, James. I want you to grow up and not get high all day long. Sue me. Come home and have a beer to relax like an adult. You shouldn't have to go to outer space to wind down."

"Half a joint and a baseball game is hardly on the moon, Maye. Don't exaggerate. We've gotten high together a million times!"

"Try twice, honey. Now who's the exaggerator? Not to mention; that was before we were parents."

"Foster parents," specified Jim.

"Well, I've kind of been meaning to talk to you about that," Maye said timidly.

"Oh no. Don't start with that again, Maye," Jim said, rubbing his eyes in frustration. "I'm trying to listen to the game." He turned the radio up.

"We are going to have to talk about it eventually, Jim. I mean, he's been with us for how many months now? They still haven't found him parents yet."

"Two. It's been two months. Fifty-six days to be exact. It was the last time you let me smoke. Isn't Dr. Darlington the 'they' that's supposed to be finding the kid a home? Is he even looking? I still don't even fully understand his connection either. I thought he was the chancellor or something of that private school?"

"He's the headmaster of Lindinium Prep and capable of handling multiple responsibilities at once," Maye said, crossing her arms and turning up her nose. "You could take a lesson or two, babe!"

"Do you mean like how he found Pete a home in the first place?" said Jim. "Look, at the end of the day, he's a great kid, but we aren't ready. Money is tight enough as it is, even with what the state pays us for fostering Pete. You know I'm going to be out of work when the lake starts to freeze over. School clothes, Christmas and birthday presents … they all cost money, Maye! What if he wants to play hockey one day? Do you know how fucking expensive youth hockey is?"

"Jim, you're talking about one day like it's tomorrow. Besides, he's tall for his age. And in case you hadn't noticed, he's Black. He'll probably play basketball anyhow. We've got time, baby! We'll be fine off of your unemployment over the winter and you're such a hard worker I know that you'll get promotions and raises up the wazoo! I can help, too! Joanne started selling Mary Kay and is raking it in, she tells me. I can do that!"

"Mary Kay?" asked Jim.

"Sure! What's so hard about selling makeup? Every girl wants to be pretty, right? My father outsold every other salesman at Bristol Myers for 22 years. He did just as well with curtain rings and insurance. I'm his daughter; it's in my blood."

"I don't think the sales gene is hereditary."

"There is only one way to find out," Maye said quickly. Pausing, she added, "But you're right. We don't need to talk about this now."

Maye got up from the couch, grabbed a dining room chair and brought it to the kitchen cabinets above the sink.

"What are you doing?" asked Jim.

She reached up and pulled a sandwich bag from the space between the cabinets and the ceiling. "I don't give you enough credit, Jim. I'm sorry. You've been really good about not smoking." Maye said, extending the baggie to Jim as she walked back into the living room. "Fifty-six days is a long time! You deserve a treat!"

"Is that what I think it is?" asked Jim with a smile.

"I pinched a little bit of your last bag of dope for a rainy day." Maye said proudly. "Let's get Pizza Hut and rent a couple movies from Video Vision! New releases are ninety-nine cents tonight. You can smoke a joint and listen to the rest of your game in the car on the way."

Jim was a bit miffed about Maye pinching his stash but happy not to have the conversation that would eventually evolve into a fight, which Jim feared he'd inevitably lose. Maye definitely inherited the sales gene from her father. She could be as charismatic and persuasive as she needed to be, and Jim was too in love to put up a respectable fight if there was something Maye wanted. He accepted any and every win he could eek out. Like smoking weed before he got home from work in the evenings for the past fifty-six days.

There was a "late ship delivery," according to Jim, which caused him to stay and work late every night over the past two months. He had a routine of pulling over and smoking a joint outside of his car before pulling into his driveway. A smoking flannel he wore over his work shirt and bottle of cool water cologne to mask the smell; Clear Eyes eye drops to get rid of the red eye; and a pack of wintergreen tic-tacs occupied the trunk of Jim's Ford Tempo to aid in hiding his habit.

Jim passed by Pete and Gwendoline playing on his way to the car. They were singing and stomping around, holding their lower backs with one hand and tapping large sticks against the ground with their other hand.

"What are you two weirdos up to?" asked Jim.

"*Old man …*" sang Pete.

"*Old lady!*" sang Gwendoline.

"*Old man!*"

"*Old lady!*"

"*Old man; old lady,*" they sang in unison.

Jim shook his head but couldn't help but to smile. "Whatever. I'm going to get a pizza and some movies. I'll be back.

"Ooh, yes!" exclaimed Pete, pumping his tiny fist. "Can Wendy come over?"

"I don't care. You better ask your mother though, Gwendoline," said Jim.

"It would be better if Peter asked my parents," said Gwendoline, "It's harder for my mom to say no to him."

"Okay!" said Pete, taking off in a full sprint without hesitation.

"Aren't you going to go with him?" Jim asked Gwendoline as he pulled his flannel from the trunk.

"I'll catch up. Why are you putting a jacket on to drive?" asked Gwendoline. "It has to be at least 70 degrees out here; it's still hot. Who are you, Mr. Rogers?"

"Ha!" said Jim, loudly. "That was so funny I forgot to laugh!"

"No, you didn't. You laughed."

"It's called sarcasm. You shouldn't try to battle wits with adults, Gwendoline."

"Okay, well, your trunk is making your jacket stink so you probably shouldn't keep clothes in it, Mr. Hookston."

The screen door of the Darlington house slammed behind Pete as he sprinted out of it and the gravel kicked up behind Jim's tires as he peeled off, swallowing the frustration of letting an 8-year-old get the best of him. Lori reluctantly agreed to let Gwendoline attend Pete's pizza party. She expressed her reservations to Dr. Darlington after Pete ran out the door.

"How many times have I told that child to stop slamming my fucking screen door!" Lori shouted, pacing the room. "Was he born in a barn?"

Dr. Darlington sat in the well-earned groove of his Lazy Boy recliner, puffing cherry tobacco from his Sherlock pipe and rereading yesterday's edition of the Lindinium Tribune.

"He didn't leave the door open, Lorraine," he said, looking over his newspaper, "that colloquialism isn't appropriate to the situation."

"Don't correct me right now, Phillip, I swear to God! I'm pissed!"

"Are you sure this isn't about Gwendoline not wanting to walk the runway for your little fashion show?" he said, folding his newspaper with a sigh.

"It was *our* little fashion show! Every year we end our day together with her modeling all of the clothes she picked out."

She stopped pacing and directed her shouts at her husband. "She's spending too much time with that boy next door! Are you listening to me, Phil? Can you hear me from your favorite chair, or are you more concerned with rereading all the news that was barely worth reporting yesterday than with the wellbeing of your daughter?"

"Perhaps she's just growing up, dear. Isn't that what we are going for?"

Dr. Darlington rose from his chair with a grunt and walked over to the front window to stare out while he brought his point home.

"Part of that …" puffs his pipe for effect, "… is wanting to spend more time with their friends than you. Just wait until she's a teenager! But she'll come around eventually. Times is always a changin,' as they say … it's the only constant, you know."

Lori rolled her eyes.

"This better not be a sign of the times to come, Phil. Gwendoline doesn't need any distractions this coming school year. We've worked too hard for her to get ahead of the class to let her fall behind now!"

"For God's sake, Lorraine! She's in the third grade! To be technical, she isn't even in the third grade yet. Relax!"

"Don't tell me to relax. And you know I hate it when you call me Lorraine, Jr.! Loraine is my mother's name! She relaxed with me and look where I ended up."

"I didn't think about it that way. What a horrible consolation prize your daughter, and I have been!"

"Don't do that, Phil. You know what I mean. My parents were both successful and powerful lawyers. They had every resource and opportunity to pass on to me and they chose to push me into the arts instead. I spent nearly three decades of my adult life working dead end jobs and struggling while I waited for my opportunity to be the "Monet of Minnesota" or something. I asked God for the inspiration to paint a masterpiece, and he gave me a child instead. At least she still has the potential to do something great. I'll be damned if I'm the one who'll be responsible for wasting it!"

I

A year passed by with Pete living at the Hookston house. Dr. Darlington was of little help to Pete's adoption process as a case worker. He interviewed one couple that was more interested in adopting an infant with less potential baggage, but other than that, Dr. Darlington's year was spent tending to his own garden, the job he tolerated for the pension, raising his daughter, and tiptoeing around his wife's emotional landmines. He felt as if he were always babysitting. He'd even look after Pete when Maye and Jim needed a date night, which also alleviated some of the guilt from not having found Pete a permanent home yet.

Neither Jim nor Maye enjoyed the art of cooking. They preferred drive-thru cuisine and frozen dinners in front of the television over hamburger hotdish or pot roast around the dining room table. Their fast-food lifestyle grew expensive during Jim's hiatus from the Grain Silo. They let it ride and survived the winter; however, Jim got a second job that spring bussing tables on the new dinner cruise pirate ship that was docked one pier down from his main gig.

The Jolly Roger was one of the two ships in the Gitchee Gummi Pirate Experiences armada. The Vessel docked and set sail from its slip on the Lindinium side of Lake Superior in the city's tourist hotspot, The Canal Park District. It's counterpart, The Whydah, anchored down at night at the Barkers Island Marina across the bay in Superior.

Dinner service was timed to end as the ships neared each other in the middle of The Big Lake, firing pyrotechnic cannons at one another.

The battling buccaneers commandeered each other's frigates to commence in prop sword fights choreographed to clinking sounds over the ships' P.A. system. The intra pirate riffs and banter played up on the Minnesota-Wisconsin border battle. The experience concluded with both ships feeling like winners as the pirates and patrons dance and drink together on their way back to shore.

The extra cash flow kept Pete flushed with enough action figures and Disney VHS tapes to keep him occupied for the summer. Jim and Maye had fewer date nights because he was always working but the restaurants she chose got more expensive to make up for it. Jim resented having to work all the time, but he very much appreciated the feeling of being a provider. His mother, Margret, reminded him on a weekly basis of how short a distance an apple falls from the tree—in reference to Jim's father, Franklin, and his insatiable work ethic. Neither Jim nor Franklin appreciated being compared to one another. They still weren't on speaking terms if you don't include Frank rhetorically wondering where he went wrong with Jim loud enough for him to here through the phone on he and his mother's Sunday morning phone calls.

Maye loved many aspects of motherhood. The way Pete's eyes lit up every time she entered a room, access to the hangout sessions with her friends from high school that had been relegated to child birthday parties, and an excuse to watch cartoons and play silly games. However, waking up early and getting Pete ready for school in the morning wasn't a labor of love, she was well equipped to honor. They lived at the outermost edge of the school district, which meant Pete and Gwendoline were the first stop on the bus route. 5:55 a.m. every morning and not a minute later.

Their bus driver, Davey, was a retired four-star naval admiral. He served his country for forty-four years without taking time to find a wife or make babies to share his life with after retirement. Driving the bus helped the admiral pass the days and gave him somewhere else to where his service dress uniform besides on his way to the mailbox to get his pension check. The stripes and war medals pinned to Davey's jacket were always initially impressive to students who were new to his route;

however, the whispers of what happened underneath the eye patch he earned with the help of a misfired fougasse never seemed to dissipate.

Gwendoline stood alone on a chilly late September morning, waiting for the bus at the end of the driveway.

"Where's your little boyfriend today, little girl?" asked Davey, cranking open the bus doors.

"Gross out, Mr. Davey! Peter is practically a baby!"

"You're all babies to me … well … is he coming or not? Time waits for no man. Or baby."

"His mo … I mean, Mrs. Hookston … woke up late, not me! She told me to walk down ahead and wait for Peter. He's supposed to be right behind me."

"She told *you* to wait?" he asked, pointing at Gwendoline.

"Well, yes, but I think she meant for me to tell *you* to wait," she clarified.

"Do you think she meant for you to *ask* me or *tell* me?"

"Probably ask?" she shrugged.

Davey paused, "Well?"

Gwendoline sighed, "Will you wait for Peter, please?"

"No," he said quickly. "You can wait here if you'd like, but we are as of now thirty-two …thirty-three … thirty-four seconds behind schedule already. To wait for Pete wouldn't be fair to the rest of the kids who were promptly waiting and respecting other people's time. By the time I finish speaking we'll be forty seconds late. Are you coming?"

Gwendoline stalled and meandered halfway up the first stair as slowly as possible. She turned back with hopes of seeing Pete running down the driveway, just catching a glimpse of him sprinting towards her as Davey cranked the door shut in her face.

"Wendy!!! Wendy!! Wait! Here I am! I'm ready!" screamed Pete, waving his arms frantically at the yellow blur pulling off down the frontage road without him.

Pete turned around with his head hung low. It was no ordinary day of school Pete was missing that late September Friday: It was popcorn day. It costs twenty-five cents a bag. Pete hunted quarters in the couch cushions for two weeks until he found enough to bring popcorn home for everyone. Pete shook the quarters around in his pocket like dice and dragged his feet through the gravel slowly on his short walk back home.

Maye, assuming Pete made it safely on the bus, went back to sleep. Pete, upset his plans were foiled, hurled his fistful of quarters at Mayes bedroom door and began to weep. Maye was startled out of her slumber by the hollow clang of change against the faux wood door.

"What's happening?! Jim?" said Maye, flinging open the door.

Pete had already marched into the living room. He was sitting crossed legged in front of the television with an afghan draped over his head. Pete pouted with his arms folded and pretended not to hear Maye calling his name.

"Pete? Is that you underneath your blankie?"

"No!" Pete said angrily.

"Oh … I see. Do you know where I can find Pete? I thought he was on his way to school," said Maye.

"I don't know. Wherever he is, he isn't at popcorn day!" pouted Pete.

"Okay, what are you doing then? Whoever you are."

"Watching TV," Pete said bluntly.

"How can you watch TV from under a blanket, you silly goose?" said Maye as she yanked the blanket from Pete's head.

"Hey!" he shouted. "I'm listening to the TV. This is an old *David the Gnome*. I saw this one."

"It is you, Pete! Fibber! Was that you crying bloody murder in here? Why didn't you get on the bus with Gwendoline? Didn't she wait for you like I asked her to?"

"You made me miss popcorn day! Not Wendy!" screamed Pete as he began to cry again.

"Don't cry honey! What's popcorn day?" she asked.

"At school. Popcorn. Movies. All my new friends … I been sa … I been sav… I been s …s … s …" Pete stammered through his tears.

"Is that all? A little popcorn?" asked Maye.

"You don't get it. I was going to …."

"Because … we have some Act II in the cupboard," Maye said, cutting Pete off. "I can make you some popcorn, honey."

"It's not the same! Why didn't you wake up five minutes early? Abneral Davey doesn't wait for kids. What if I don't know as much as the other kids on Monday … this isn't fair!"

"I'm sorry, sweetie. I didn't mean to let you down," said Maye, holding back tears of her own. "I'm trying …."

Pete saw a tear run down Maye's cheek and felt bad for yelling.

"It's okay … I'm sorry …" said Pete grasping Maye's arm, "I can have popcorn some other time … Don't cry … you're doing a good job!"

"Thanks buddy," she said, hugging Pete. "You know something? You're pretty understanding for a five-year-old! How did you get to be so smart, mister?"

Pete shrugged his shoulders and half smiled at the compliment.

"Hey! Guess what?" asked Maye. "I have a great idea. Why don't we have our own popcorn day?"

"But we don't have *The Rescuers Down Under* tape to watch like they have at school," said Pete.

"We can watch *Ernest Goes to Jail,* again?" suggested Maye.

"Know what I mean, Vern?" replied Pete, quoting the movie.

"I'll take that as a yes," said Maye. "Then, when *The Price Is Right* comes on later, we can play along with the show and see who the best guesser is."

"That's definitely me!" he said proudly. "When I go to the grocery store with Wendy and her mom, I look at all the cans and boxes. I rememberized the numbers."

"I better be on my toes then. Go run and put on your play clothes, and I'll start the popcorn!"

"Cool! Maybe you were right. Staying home from school isn't so bad after all," Pete thought out loud.

"Don't get used to this, kiddo. This is the last day of school I'm going to let you miss. And since this is the last one, let's keep it our little secret and not tell Jim about it. He isn't as understanding as you are. Can I count on you, Secret Squirrel?"

Pete zipped his lips and threw away the imaginary key, then ran to his room to change. Unfortunately, for Pete's attendance record, it wasn't his last absence due to missing the bus. He was beginning to fall behind, so he was moved to the p.m. kindergarten class. He was sad about losing the classmates he was just starting to get used to, but had fun watching *Swamp Thing* on television with Maye the first morning, and getting to ride home with Gwendoline after school gave Pete something to look forward to throughout the day.

*****Page Break*****

Pete stood in line to board the bus home, eagerly waiting to tell Gwendoline about his first day in his new class.

"Hey, Abneral Davey!" said Pete, walking up the stairs to the bus.

"Private, we've spoken about this before," said Davey. "It's Admiral Nelson. I'm a decorated war hero, not a host for silly children's programing … That, or call me Mr. Davey."

"Yes sir!" Pete saluted Davey, then turned and marched in lockstep while scanning the occupied benches in search of his Wendy. Gwendoline was just as excited to reunite as Pete was. She waved her arms in the air and called out to him as soon as she saw his head poke above the front barrier.

"Peter! Back here! I saved you a seat!"

"No yelling on the bus!" Davey shouted.

"OH, YEAH! SORRY ABOUT THAT MR. DAVEY!" Gwendoline shouted louder deliberately.

"Hi Wendy!" Pete whispered with an ear-to-ear grin on his face. "It was my first day of school today!"

"It was your first day in a new class, not your first day of school, goofball!" she corrected, "Well ... how was it? Sit down here and tell me all about it!"

"Well, Ms. Bremerish is the same, so that's good. All the kids are different though."

"Of course they are, Peter. Different classes have different kids."

"I thought we were all going to do p.m. class. None of my friends were there," Pete said.

"You'll just have to make some more friends, Peter."

"I didn't know what anyone was talking about, and nobody asked me any questions. I don't think they want any new friends."

"That's bonkers, Peter. Who wouldn't want a new friend that is as nice as you are? Give them time to get used to you and if they still don't want to play then they can go to heck! I don't have that many friends at school … I keep to myself," Gwendoline said proudly.

"I always play by myself at home. What do you go to school for if you don't have friends to play with?"

"You don't need friends to play with at school," She assured him, "trust me, by the time you get to the fourth grade you'll be over it anyways. All the boys want to do is roughhouse, even with girls. All the girls want to do is make fun of you for wearing horses on your sweatshirts! You go to school to learn how to be a grown-up! Then you get a job, get married, have kids. And then when they have kids, you turn into a grandpa, and I'll turn into a grandma!"

"Do you mean I'll be an old man and you'll be an old lady? I'd rather play the game instead. Start it off, Wendy!"

"I'm not singing that song in front of everyone on the bus, and you don't have a choice; you don't get to play games when you grow up."

"That sounds dumb," Pete said, slouching. "Also, we are sitting behind everyone, not in front of them. They won't even notice."

"It's super dumb; but someone has to do grown-up stuff. My father complained about raking the leaves all day yesterday, but he still does it all the time."

"What's so bad about that? You get to jump in the pile!"

"I don't think my dad even knows how to jump," Gwendoline thought out loud. "He doesn't like games. He's always too busy balancing his checkbook and stuff."

"Let's jump in the leaves when we get home!" Pete declared.

Gwendoline happily obliged his suggestion. The two of them could barely contain themselves for the rest of the ride home. They ran past Davey shouting at them to slow down and kept that pace going all the way down the driveway. Pete and Gwendoline flung their backpacks along with all of their caution into the wind the moment their feet touched the grass of their shared side lawn.

The crimson and carnelian mounds of fallen leaves that Dr. Darlington spent the greater portion of the previous day raking never stood a chance. Pete and Gwendoline dove in with belly flops and rolled over to make angels on their backs. The sound of laughter and rustling leaves traveled into the open window of Lori's studio, interrupting the artistic flow she was about to enter.

"Gwendoline Marie Darlington! Do you think your father spent all day yesterday raking these leaves to build you delinquents a playland?" shouted Lori, walking outside as the screen door slammed behind her.

"Maybe?" Gwendoline asked coyly.

Jim pulled up the driveway home from work early that day. He'd taken the night off from the Jolly Roger to look after Pete so Maye could attend a Mary Kay facial party.

"Don't play dumb with me, young lady. Dust yourself off and get into the house. I want you to get your homework done quickly so you can bag up these leaves before supper is ready. You and Peter can play after that; if there is time." said Lori.

"But Peter ...."

"But nothing! I don't see Peter out here not doing what he's supposed to be doing!"

"I don't see Peter out here at all, now that you mention it!" said Jim as he walked towards Lori and Gwendoline. "Where is that little partner in crime of yours? Don't tell me he'd rather be inside watching TV than out here playing with you."

"What?" asked Gwendoline.

"You know … Pete … my foster kid … about yay tall?" Jim said, waving his hand beside his waist.

"I know who Peter is; I don't know where Peter is, though,"

"What do you mean you don't know where Pete is?!? Wasn't he supposed to start riding home on the bus with you today?" asked Jim.

"Maybe he took a different bus by accident?" suggested Gwendoline. "Or maybe he missed it altogether? You know Mr. Davey, Mr. Hookston; he's leaving on time, with or without you."

"Who the hell is Davey? Jesus Christ does Maye at least know where Pete is?" asked Jim.

"Maye is already gone, Jim," said Lori. "She asked me to keep an eye on Peter until you ..."

"Booya!" Pete sprung up from the pile of leaves he was hiding in like a stripper out of a giant birthday cake, startling both Jim and Lori. Pete pumped his fists in celebration. Gwendoline laughed hysterically.

"We got 'em, Wendy! They didn't even know I was in there!" Pete boasted.

"I knew where he was the whole time," Lori said, defending herself.

"Sure, you did, mother," Gwendoline said sarcastically. "Why did you jump?"

"I didn't jump until he did," Lori said, pointing at Jim. "Don't worry about it. Worry about not getting into trouble. Go pick up your knapsack and meet me at the dining room table to go over what I'd like you to work on this evening."

"Ughh, fine!" Gwendoline got up off of the ground, brushed herself off, then extended her hand to help Pete up. They high-fived each other as they parted ways towards their respective houses.

"I can't wait to tell Maye how good we got you guys!" Pete said to Jim as they walked up the front sidewalk.

"It's a good thing she wasn't home yet. Otherwise, she'd see you didn't take the time to change into your play clothes before getting dirty. I don't think she appreciates having to scrub and wash the new school clothes I just bought you," Jim said.

"That's why I wore my play clothes to school this morning! Once something is dirty it can't get more dirtier!" Pete said confidently.

"Eh, well … nevermind. Sure. Are you telling me that Maye dressed you in those dirt-stained green corduroys and sent you out into the world like this?"

"She didn't see them, but I know she doesn't like to wash clothes, so I thought I was helping. She said she wasn't feeling good and went back to bed before I got on the bus."

Jim shook his head, "Well, at least you went to school, bud. Way to be a big kid. Maye was feeling sick again, huh? It's funny how she miraculously felt better in time to go to her Mary Kay thing. What a hypochondriac!"

"What's that?" asked Pete.

"It's when you think that you're sick but you're really not," Jim said.

"Is it like make-believe?"

"Exactly, my boy! It's make-believe!"

"That sounds like a dumb game …"

"You're telling me …"

❚❚

"Thank you for taking me to the doctor, Joanne. And thank you for letting me bitch to you for hours afterward as well," Maye said to her friend. They sat parked in front of Maye's house after what she told Jim was a Mary Kay party.

"You betcha, Mayflower. I'm happy to be here for you! I'll call you tomorrow afternoon to find out the test results, okay?"

"Uhm … no. I mean, no need to worry. It could be tomorrow or a few days. Maybe I won't hear back from the doctor at all and that means everything is fine! Fine and benign! Ha! No news is good news, am I right?" Maye said with nervous laughter.

"Nonsense. They have to call you!" said Joanne, shaking her head emphatically. "Your mother died of cancer for heaven's sake! They have to know the emotional toll of waiting by the phone to find out if *you* have cancer! You can pretend to be calm about this all you want, but you wouldn't have called me to take you into urgent care if you weren't worried. I'm going to call you every hour, on the hour, starting bright and early, until we know for sure that you are cancer-free!"

"You really don't have to do that, Jo. I appreciate your concern, but I'll call you. No sense in worrying about something I can't control. I don't want to tell Jim until I have to, either; I don't want him to worry for no reason."

Maye fixed her game face on the way up the sidewalk to walk in the front door with level eleven energy. "There my boys are!" Maye exclaimed, extending her arms for a hug from Pete.

Pete sprang up excitedly from his seat in front of the television. He was watching one of his favorite VHSs at the time, *Harry and the*

Henderson's. Jim was sitting on the couch, enjoying a beer while he listened to the game and plucked at his guitar.

"Hey honey, did you sell all of your make-up tonight?" asked Jim.

"Very funny, honey. May I at least kick my shoes off and sit down before you make fun of me?" asked Maye.

"That question was mostly optimistic," said Jim. "You don't have your gigantic case that seems to be filled with more stuff every time you leave the house with it. I was hoping for the opposite to be true."

"Oh, you're right. I don't have it. I must have left it in Joanne's back seat," she said. "I have to buy more products if I want to sell more products, Jim. That's how sales work."

"Don't you mean, *I* have to buy more products so *you* can sell more products?" Jim clarified. "That might be a viable sales strategy if you actually had someone to sell to. All of your friends sell Mary Kay as well, and none of them are driving a pink Cadillac but Joanne. Phil even said it was a pyramid scheme."

"Hydrooooo cul-de-sac!" Pete yelled as he broke free from Maye's hug. Pete was playing superhero before taking a movie break. He was wearing Batman briefs over his onesie and a cape made from his blankie, which had a hole in it large enough for Pete to stick his head through. He ran to mount himself on the arm of the couch, opposite Jim, then leapt to the love seat as if he were flying.

"What did he say, Jim?" asked Maye.

"Like I ever know?" said Jim, grateful that Pete couldn't yet pronounce hypochondriac. Probably someone Batman fights. Just have to go with it, right?"

Maye sat down on the couch, curling up next to Jim.

"How was your day today, Baby?" she asked.

"It's going to be a great night if Jack and Kirby can bring us another World Series!" said Jim.

"Isn't *this* great, Jim?" asked Maye.

"Isn't what great?"

"This. Our little family! Me, you, Pete. We have it all. Don't we?"

"Of course, babe: But it's game seven. Please … not right now."

"Okay. Okay, fine, said Maye. "Listen to your game. I'll leave you alone. Hey, Pete, how was your day, little Mr.?"

Pete was weeping quietly as he sat in front of the television, watching his movie. He turned around with glistening eyes but didn't say anything.

"What's the matter, Pete? Did something happen at school today?" asked Maye.

"Pete's fine, Maye," Jim laughed, "He's crying about the movie, that's all. He gets sad every time Harry has to go back into the woods, no matter how many times we've had to watch it. Like Bigfoot is real or something; it's hilarious!"

"It's not funny!" Pete shouted.

"Don't raise your voice at me!" Jim scolded.

"Don't make fun of him, Jim!" said Maye.

"Harry doesn't know why he can't stay with his new family. He's sad!" said Pete.

"See what I mean?" Jim laughed even harder. "Even if Sasquatch existed, he wouldn't get sad about a family. Harry would have eaten the family in the first act and the movie is over."

"It's okay, Pete. It's only a movie," assured Maye. "Why don't you go play superhero again? I think I saw the… Hydrocoldasac run into your room. You better go save the city!" she continued.

Pete stood up, wiped his eyes, and planted his fists firmly into his hips. "Crime always needs fightin' I guess!"

He ran towards his room, somersaulted through the doorway, then kicked the door closed behind him.

"Was that necessary, Jim? He's only five!"

"Yeah, a soft five," scoffed Jim.

"A soft five, James? Did you ever stop to think that maybe he relates to Harry?"

"It's a Yeti!" declared Jim. "How can he possibly see himself in a creature of myth?"

"They both feel like they don't have a permanent home or something. I don't know … abandonment issues?" suggested Maye.

"You sound like Phil with that psychobabble bullshit! Kids can't comprehend shit like that. Especially one who lives in the clouds as much as he does!"

"So what? Pete has a silly imagination, and the boy is a little sensitive. He's been through a lot. He's in school and making friends now. I don't know what he would do without Gwendoline! Pete has a life here that he loves. I'm sure he's scared it's going to be taken away from him again."

Maye and Jim argued back and forth over what quickly escalated to the subject of Pete's adoption. Pete Eavesdropped from the hallway. He hated watching them quarrel but was too curious of a child not to listen. He found an effective method of peacemaking over time by tugging at his foster parents' waists and asking them to "stop fussin" with cute vitriol.

"That isn't going to work this time, Pete. I thought we told you to go play in your room?" said Jim, unwilling to entertain the bit.

The crack of a baseball snapped Jim's attention to the sound of an excited announcer calling the end of the baseball game.

"The Twins are going to win the World Series! … The Twins have won it! It's a base hit … it's a one-nothing … ten innings …."

"Oh great! I missed it! I got to listen to the Braves walk Kirby Puckett and Ken Hrbek, sure, but I missed the ending!" Jim whined. "Can't wait to go to work and talk about the game, 'Oh, hey there, Jim. Hell of a game last night, huh? Where were you when Gene Larkin hit the game-winning single to make baseball history?' 'I missed it, Bob! I heard Jack Morris throw his eighth strikeout after refusing to come out of the game, but at the moment the Twins won game seven of the World Series in extra innings, I'm happy to say I was trying to convince my foster kid that he's not a fucking Wendigo!'"

"And look at you still breathing!" said Maye. "I'll be sure not to interrupt you next time you're listening to someone else achieve something great. I wouldn't want to blow another chance at being a part of history for you!'"

Pete ran into his room, slamming the door behind him.

"Look what you did, now!" Maye scolded. "What's a Wendigo?"

"It's like an Indian Bigfoot … I think."

"Pete!" Gwendoline said, standing above Pete as he lie asleep in bed. "What are you still doing asleep?!? Look outside!" she shook him awake and pointed out Pete's bedroom window.

"What are you supposed to be?" asked Pete, rubbing the sleep from his eyes.

Gwendoline was bundled head to toe in winter gear. Her snowsuit was so thick her walk was closer to a waddle and her arms were suspended at her side like a starfish. The homemade knit scarf wrapped around her neck stopped just before her eyes. Her hat draped just below her brow and the fuzzy ball hanging from the top of it swung wildly as she coaxed Peter out of bed and over to the window.

"This isn't my Halloween costume, you dweeb! It's a snowsuit … to play outside … it's a fudging snow day!!!" Gwendoline said giddily.

Lindinium was in the early stages of a record breaking, two-day snowstorm. The blizzard brought nearly thirty-seven inches of snow in total over the next forty-eight hours. However, the aching pain of shoveling their cars out of banks created by the snowplows clearing the streets lingered in the lower backs of Northern Minnesotans for weeks. All Gwendoline could think about that morning was a day off from school.

"Holy cow! Look at all of it! There is snow up to the third stair of the treehouse! Did I sleep 'til Christmas?" Pete asked, watching the snow fall in awe with his hands pressed against the glass.

"It's actually a rung, not a stair, Pete. And it's impossible to sleep that long unless you are a bear," Gwendoline said. "But I guess you could say that today is a gift! No school! Isn't that awesome?"

"No school? Why not? Snow is *outside*!"

"I don't think you heard me … We don't have to go to school today." said Gwendoline, enunciating slowly through cupped hands. "It's the one day where there is nothing else to do but play … and you want to go to school? You're an odd duck, Peter."

"I was going to go to school dressed up as Batman, not Howie the Duck!" said Pete. "Everyone was going to love me in my costume; now they will never get to see it."

The day after Jim and Maye's World Series blowout, Jim bought Pete a vinal Batman costume to smooth things over. Pete tried it on and went to Gotham in his brain. He would have worn it every day until Halloween if he were allowed to.

"Put it on over your snowsuit. Who gives a care?" Gwendoline said.

Pete smiled and ran into the dining room to ask where his snowsuit from last winter was. Jim was sitting at the table sipping coffee with a little Baileys in it, tuning his guitar up to jam away the snow day he was also grateful to have been gifted.

"Have you seen my snowsuit?" Pete asked, pressing on Jim's guitar strings to hold his attention.

"I saw you outgrow it last winter, remember?" said Jim, removing his guitar strap with frustration. "You don't have a snowsuit yet."

"My mom makes sure to buy all my winter clothes in the spring, and a size too big, so I have room to grow into them. You should have thought ahead, Mr. Hookston," said Gwendoline.

"There were a lot of things I couldn't have seen coming last spring--a snowstorm in October being one of them." Jim said, deadpan.

"What am I supposed to do? I don't get to play outside?" asked Pete.

"Oh, shit. Here comes the water works. Are you going to cry now?" Jim asked Pete. "Maye?" Jim shouted, summoning his wife who was still slumbering soundly.

"I'm not crying! I'm a big kid," Pete replied.

"There you go! Big kids don't need snowsuits," Jim said.

"Wendy has a snowsuit," Pete said.

"Yeah, but Wendy is a girl. You're a boy, Pete. You are supposed to be tougher than that. My old man was too much of a tightwad to buy me snow gear, so I made do. Lots of layers and grocery bags always suited me just fine."

"Grocery bags?" Pete and Gwendoline asked simultaneously.

"Sure!" said Jim. "You put them on your feet and tie them up tightly around your ankles to keep your socks from getting wet. Pretty neat trick, huh? Go and wake Maye up so she can help you get ready."

"Can't you just help me?" asked Pete.

"Yeah. Mrs. Hookston is still sleeping," said Gwendoline. "You were just pretending to play guitar like you do every other day."

"Well, little miss from the cheap seats, today is a rare, paid day off I intend to take full advantage of. Something my wife takes full advantage of every other day. It's my turn to relax."

Maye layered Pete with sweatpants, two pairs of jeans, three crew neck sweatshirts and four pairs of socks covered in plastic grocery bags from the Super Value store over his footed onesie. Pete put his coat on then shimmied into his Halloween costume, stretching the vinal seams of the cheap getup to their limits. After he donned his Batman mask atop Jim's oversized three-hole ski mask, Pete mashed his feet into his boots, slipped on a thin pair of gloves, then mittens, and stood eagerly next to the front door.

"Do I look warm?" asked Pete, presenting himself to Jim.

Jim smiled and nodded. "Boy, I remember my snow days back in Lindstrom. You kids have it easy nowadays with the little thing on the bottom of the screen telling you when school is canceled. You even have a number to call that tells you the time and weather. I had to listen to the radio early in the morning until I heard them say Chisago Lakes was closed for the day."

"Cool story, Mr. Hookston," Gwendoline said, rolling her eyes. "Are you going to get dressed and play with us since you have a snow day here in Lindinium? My dad is. He has to because he can't think of a better excuse."

"Yeah. Everyone is going to play!" assured Pete.

"Yeah, Jim. Everyone is going to play!" said Maye, walking out of her bedroom bundled for the elements. "You don't have a better excuse either."

Jim pretended to agree reluctantly; however, he was secretly just as giddy to play in the snow as the children were. He couldn't resist an opportunity to flex the snow fort-building prowess he prided himself on as a child. The blue ribbons his prized structures won from the annual Celebration of Lakes Winterfest snow sculpture contest have been nailed to the mantle above the fireplace in his parents' home since the mid-seventies.

"I used to be the king at building snow forts!" Jim boasted. "We are going to make a fort so strong you couldn't knock it over with a bulldozer. I'll let the two of you fight about who gets to use it during the snowball war."

"I'm the queen of snow angels," added Maye. "I'll teach you how to make a perfect angel and get up without leaving a handprint!"

Everyone was properly bundled and on their way out the door when the phone rang.

"I'll get it." said Jim, chomping down on his glove to remove it. "It's probably my manager from the Jolly Roger officially calling me off for my night shift."

"No, Jim. I'll get it," insisted Maye, fearing it might be the doctors. "You go start the fort with the kids. It's probably Joanne, anyways."

"Telephone, Jim. It's your job." yelled Maye as she walked out the door thirty seconds later.

"I told you …" he yelled back.

"Yellow?" said Jim to the voice on the phone.

"James Hookston? This is Maurice Secondstar, chairman of the RBC. I believe we met briefly at your J.R. orientation."

As chairman of the Reservation Business Committee, Maurice directed the operations of all reservation-run facilities, determined approval status of all new business and construction in Gawikaki, and had major influence in the allocation of tribal reparation funds. Like his Grandfather, the great Chief Victor Secondstar, Maurice had a deeply rooted love and dedication for his tribe. He showed his love and dedication by treating every potential dollar earned as if it were a stone in the foundation of the community, he was responsible for setting up to thrive.

"Oh, sure!" said Jim after thinking for a moment. "What can I do for you, Mo?"

"You can start by never calling me Mo again, son. I'll let it slide this time; if you'll tell me that you can work today."

"Work? Today?" Jim asked holding back frustration. "The storm of the century is brewing outside, sir! I've covered that song by Gordon Lightfoot; it can't be safe to go out there."

"Of course not. No ship of mine is going to go down like the Fitzgerald. It is, however, Halloween. And being snowed in with nothing else to do is a perfect reason for them to party and for me to make all the money every business that closed down won't. We are going to remain docked and open the bar for snowmobilers and hotel guests around the ship. Can I count on you, James?" asked Chairman Secondstar.

"Gee, sir, I'd love to help out the team but I'm just a busboy. I don't know anything about bartending."

"Beggars can't be choosers. This is an emergency; you can learn on the job. We'll all know that you don't know what you are doing so it doesn't matter if you fuck up. The customers will be grateful just to have an open place to drink the storm out no matter what kind of service they get. You know how to drink, don't you?"

"I'm a quick learner," Jim said, burping up Baily's.

"That's funny. You're clever too, a natural," said Chairman Secondstar.

"I appreciate your faith in me, Mr. Secondstar, but I couldn't get down to Canal Park even if I wanted to. I'm way out in the sticks and my car won't even make it down the driveway."

"Well, that's one of the reasons I called you. I'm looking at your file, here, and … as luck would have it, I live close by!"

Bully for me, thought Jim twirling his finger in the air,

"I have a truck with four-wheel drive and a big ass plow hanging from the grill. I will come and pick you up. Be ready in twenty minutes unless you have another excuse in your busser apron?"

Jim was off to work and everyone else got to playing. Even Lori made a willing and gleeful appearance to add artistic blotches of blue and red food coloring to Dr. Darlington's snowman, or "snow-bland," as she called it. Maye and Gwendoline made snow angels while Pete searched for the perfect snowbank to build a fort that would impress Jim when he got home. He found it underneath the treehouse.

Pete leapt from the highest rung of the treehouse that Maye would allow him into a tall drift he believed to be a snowbank. He sank to the bottom and burrowed himself out, laughing hysterically the whole time. So much so he didn't notice his costume ripped on the way out. He returned to the drift with a garden spade to carve out a tunnel in which to hide with premade snowballs until someone came looking for him.

"You haven't made your angel yet, Pete. Where are you?," Maye called.

She poked her head into the top hole of Pete's snow fort and was greeted with a snowball to the face. She answered Pete with a light whitewashing. The Darlington's made their way over to investigate the ensuing laughter, only to be greeted with an onslaught of unexpected flying powder. They all ran around the yard like children, pelting each other with snow until falling to catch snowflakes with their eye lids. The echoes of their belly laughter flowed throughout the woods surrounding them.

As fun as the afternoon was, the adults suggested a break in the action to warm up. Only Pete and Gwendoline had any real intention to go back outside. Dr. Darlington retired to his study. Lori invited Maye over for coffee and Baileys to expedite the thawing process. She made hot cocoa on the stove for the kids and brought it to them in the living room while they warmed their toes underneath the radiator.

"Ooh, is that Cool Whip?" Pete asked as Lori approached wielding warm beverages.

"Of course!" Lori said.

"And the baby marshmallows?" asked Gwendoline.

"*Are there miniature marshmallows in the hot chocolate?*" asked Lori, correcting Gwendoline's grammar.

"How should I know? That's why I was asking you, duh!" replied Gwendoline.

"You can still lose your treat, young lady," warned Lori.

Gwendoline paused as if she were swallowing her pride. "I beg of your pardon, mother dearest. Are there any miniature marshmallows in our hot cocoa?" Gwendoline asked sarcastically.

Lori didn't appreciate the sass. Nor did she appreciate both Pete and Maye being entertained by Gwendoline's antics.

"What are you laughing at, Peter?" Lori asked in a snotty tone.

"Wendy's funny accent," he answered.

"Who is Wendy? That is a horrid nickname!" Lori said with disgust.

"Mom, it's not that bad and you've heard Peter call me that a bunch of times," defended Gwendoline.

"I didn't appreciate it any other time I've heard it previously, either. I named you Gwendoline. Not Wendy. Not Gwen. And definitely not Lynn …"

"Lighten up, Lorraine," said Dr. Darlington as he exited the room.

"They know I'm kidding," said Lori waving off her husband. "We were having fun. Why don't you go back into your nursery and play with Ken Burns, Jr."

Jim came home later that evening with to-go boxes full of chicken wings and onion rings, a solid buzz, and a promise of promotion when the snow melted next spring. He and Maurice Secondstar drank Old Styles and spiced rum while they shot the breeze waiting for customers to show up. Jim didn't have much opportunity to prove himself as a bartender but his willingness to work, seasoned with a good deal of inebriated face time with the boss, proved Jim to be worthy of a future barback position. Financially, it was a slight bump in tip-outs and one step closer to a full-time position somewhere higher up in the company with benefits and a future, as Chairman Secondstar promised.

A summer job on the Jolly Roger was far more enjoyable than hauling grain at dawn, and the joy he felt from working so close to the water was intensified to the umpteenth power when the Jolly Roger set sail. Jim felt the majesty radiating from the middle of Lake Superior under the moonlight. He would steal moments between courses when he could, to stare at the deep purple horizon from the employee smoking deck on the back of the ship. Jim went there to breathe in a few pulls from his one-hitter, as well as to imagine what his future could be one day. He also enjoyed a drag or two from an Auerbach Red here and there if a coworker offered him a cigarette.

Often times Jim pictured himself fishing alone, peacefully and far away from the sightline of the shore. Other times he saw himself with a half dozen tourists on a charter he was leading with his own boat. Lake Superior Hookers was at the top of the list for business names--if he didn't use it as a band name first, that is. Either way, he was on the water again and that was close enough to his dream for the moment.

I

Maye let the phone ring and threw out letters from her doctor's office until they stopped coming. She was too busy chasing her dream of being a mother to focus on her impending fate in real life. Maye pressed the issue relentlessly and her wish to be a mother was granted by Christmas that year. Her father, Chuck, flew in from Boca to complete her perfect family portrait and continue their longstanding tradition of Christmases at the Darlington's, which now included Jim and Pete.

Maye only intended to hold off learning of her diagnosis until after the holiday polaroids were developed and framed, but time slipped away from her. She knew in her heart that the doctor wouldn't have been blowing her up for no reason; however, she also knew that no one in their right mind would allow someone to adopt a child while actively fighting cancer, dying or not. The joy of motherhood and the fear of acknowledging death kept Maye smiling through her constant fatigue and nausea until March.

Maye would have slept most of her days away that winter had Jim not been on hiatus from work. Jim was naturally an early riser and, without a job to go to in the mornings, he had nowhere to be. Still, he was insistent that Maye be the one to ready Pete for the day each morning. He'd pace the length of the driveway, smoking as much weed as possible before waking up Maye so she could wake up Pete, who was often already awake but waiting in bed to be woken up. Pete loved the song and dance of kisses and tickles, with which Maye accosted him while he pretended to sleep.

Pete couldn't tell the time yet, however, one day, it felt as if he'd lingered in bed for much longer than normal. Near the point of giving up on the bit, he heard footsteps moving briskly down the hallway outside of his room. Pete readied himself by curling up under his Ninja Turtle comforter in a fetal position, biting his cheeks to keep himself from smiling. The footsteps kept stomping past his door. The next sounds Pete heard were coughing, gagging and violent vomiting coming from the bathroom.

"Are you okay, Mom?" Pete asked, poking his head in the bathroom doorway.

"I'm fine, sweetie. Go play, okay?" she said with her head resting on the toilet seat. "I'll be out in a little while."

"But ... you're ralphing … and you're putting your face where our butts go."

"I wish I were ralphing, honey …" said Maye, interrupting herself with a dry heave. "Nothing's coming up."

"Well ... why?"

"I don't know, honey."

"Are you sick? When people throw up, it's because they're sick …."

"Then I must be sick, Pete. Please go watch TV. I'll let you know when it's time to get ready for school."

Exhausted from being berated with obvious questions from Pete while she violently hacked up nothing but stomach acid, Maye went back to bed. Pete made himself a bowl of King Vitamin cereal and took to his favorite spot in front of the TV to watch *Eureka's Castle. Maya The Bee* played next. When that was over, Pete knew it was time to get dressed and go wait for the bus.

Pete popped into his mom's bedroom to say goodbye before he left for school. Maye couldn't hear him over the sound of her own snoring and that worried Pete. He stayed home to look after her. Pete got a row of saltines from the pantry and a can of Schweppes Ginger Ale from the fridge, then placed them on Maye's nightstand. He turned on the television before hopping into bed beside her. The old console T.V. in Jim and Maye's bedroom didn't have cable, so Pete turned the dials until a clear picture came through.

An episode of his Nonah's favorite soap opera, *Forever Young*, was playing. Pete hadn't seen the program in quite a while, however, not much had progressed in the storyline. Dr. Vance Dexter was still falling in love with whoever that week's beautiful amnesia patient used to be, before the traumatic brain injuries that somehow left their faces unblemished. Maye was still sawing logs as the end credits rolled. Pete felt her forehead to check for a fever; it was warm but not hot, so he went outside to play for a while.

It was 45 degrees by early afternoon that day. Balmy for Minnesota in March. The temperature is relative in the Northland; after spending two months in subzero temperatures, it doesn't take much to make you happy. It's running-errands-in-basketball-shorts-and-a-hoodie-weather. Stuff-your-jacket-in-your-backpack-on-the-way-home-from-school type weather. For Pete, it was slip-on-your-hat-and-gloves-to-play-outside-in-a-t-shirt-and-make-snowballs kind of weather.

The snow on the ground was plentiful but partially melted, dirty, and riddled with twigs. It was jagged and loose like a chocolate snow cone; however, it could still be forged into an unforgivingly solid snowball capable of breaking the skin when proper heat and pressure is applied. Pete made several to store in an old red cooler he found in the garage then hauled his arsenal to the lookout post he designated to be inside of the treehouse.

The illusion of warmth dissipates quickly when you stop moving. Pete sat shivering, waiting for enemy lines to encroach his territory for twenty minutes before relinquishing his post to go inside and warm up. As Pete reached the front door, he heard a car rolling slowly over the driveway gravel. It was Jim coming home from summer staff orientation on The Jolly Roger. Pete tried to run back to his post in the treehouse before being seen but it was too late.

"Pete?" Jim yelled, getting out of his car.

"Rats!" said Pete. "You weren't supposed to see me!"

"What are you doing home from school already, buddy?"

"Saving snowballs."

"No, I meant why are you home from … saving snowballs for what, Pete?' Jim asked reluctantly.

"To throw at people; duh!" Pete said, throwing his arms in the air.

"You made snowballs out of this junk?"

"Yup! All you gotta do is press it real tight in your gloves until it gets hard enough to make a ball," explained Pete.

"You said a lot more than you realize there, kiddo; but what you made sounds like an ice ball. Are you trying to hurt somebody?"

Jim reached into the backseat, grabbing a thin stack of orientation papers, his new red and white striped barback pirate shirt, and a large fast-food bag. He and Pete continued to talk as they walked up the sidewalk.

"No. I just thought it would be funny to wait until all the snow melts then hit people with snowballs."

"Well, funny is funny; I can't argue with that. I don't think it's going to work, though, Pete. How will you keep them from melting until then?"

"In the cooler you bring lunch to your work in," said Pete, proud of his ingenuity.

"You have to think things through a little further sometimes, buddy. I'm going to need that for my lunch when I go back to work."

"I thought all the snow will melt before the boats come in."

"Oh, really?" asked Jim. "Do they read you the shipping schedule on the PBS Kid's Club?"

"Nope. They say happy birthday to all the kids that have birthdays, though. I hope they say happy birthday to me this year."

"All kids have birthdays, Pete. Only kids with parents that pay money to have that furry blue thing wish their kids happy birthday get to be Channel 8 famous. As far as all this snow melting is concerned, well … we'll be lucky if the banks are gone by your birthday. Doesn't matter anyways. The icebreakers should be coming out any day now and I'll be back to work in … wait a minute, why am I explaining this to a five-year-old? Explain to me why you aren't in school!"

"Mom is sick," said Pete. "I stayed home to take care of her."

"It never ends with her!" complained Jim. "I don't know how running around outside without a jacket on is helping anyone but yourself to catch pneumonia, but it was a real big-kid move on your part to try and help out, so I'll let you off the hook … this time," Jim winked cheekily. "You still should have went to school, though."

"I'll go tomorrow," Pete said nonchalantly, "what's in the bag?"

"Do you mean this one with McDonald's written on it?" Jim asked sarcastically. "Sizzler steaks."

"Sizzler snakes?" asked Pete.

"Sizz … Never mind." Jim sighed, "Yes, Pete. There is McDonald's in the McDonald's bag."

"What about my Fish-O-Fillet Happy Meal and toy?"

"Same as every McDonalds Monday," Jim said as he opened the front door for Pete to walk in before him. "I was going to pop your food in the old micro when you got home from school, but we might as well all eat together since you're here now. Run in and wake your mom and I'll set up the food on the coffee table and put on a movie."

■■

"Yellow?" said Jim, answering the telephone.

"How about green?" said the man on the phone.

"I beg your pardon?" said Jim.

"You said, 'Yellow,' so I said, 'How about green?'" said the man. "I thought perhaps that's how the young people greet each other these days. I stopped trying to understand the changing times long ago, but I still try my damnedest to keep up with them!"

"What? No," said Jim. "I didn't say the word yellow; I said hello … just cooler … never mind. Who is this?"

"It's Chuck, ya uptight son of a bitch! You don't recognize your own father-in-law's voice?"

"Sorry about that, Mr. Hookston. How are you?"

"I'll tell you what, I'd be better if you would respect the rules of the house that I gave you. I don't bring that up to hold it over your head. I was happy to help you kids start your life together. I definitely don't want you to feel like you owe me anything either … it's your house now. However, the least you could do is respect my one and only wish. Do you know what that one rule is, James?"

"Call you Dad?" asked Jim.

"Call me Dad! That's all that I ask, Jimmy boy!"

"Ok Dad, what can I do for you today?"

"Just calling to check on my princess, that's all. I meant to call sooner but my pal Sid and I met a couple of ex-Rockettes on the back nine at Boca Lago. I felt a little guilty at first, but I'm a man, damn it. And we all grieve in our own way. Am I right, Jimbo? Anyways, how is Maye handling the day?"

"Oh, you know, sick and dying of something like any other day," said Jim.

"Watch it, now, Son. Any other day I'd laugh at that. I know my daughter can be a lot sometimes, but you have to give her today. It's always been a tough one for her."

"What's today?"

"It's March 4th. The day my Lynnie bear left Maye and I for the great above--thirteen years ago."

"Shit! Is that today?" asked Jim.

"It is indeed. I'm sure she's fine, but she's been this way since she was eleven. She used to get sick whenever she was scared to do something. Most days you can pay her no mind, and she'll feel better in an hour, but on days like today you have to lean into it. I bust your chops a lot, but I know you're a good husband. You just have to be a better one, for one day."

"How am I supposed to do that?" asked Jim.

"Sell it, Son. Sell it. Make her believe that you believe her. Has she mentioned going to see Dr. Franko today?"

"Surprisingly, no," said Jim. "She hasn't mentioned going to the hospital at all lately. Not even for a bi-annual checkup."

"Perfect," said Chuck. "Offer to take her. No. Better yet, insist she see a doctor immediately. You'll get brownie points for your concern, and she'll get a little peace of mind hearing a doctor tell her that she's fine."

"What about next time she needs attention?" asked Jim. "Won't I have to pretend I believe her every time she says the sky is falling?"

Chuck uttered a sound somewhere between a grunt and a sigh, "Yyyuuupp! That's marriage, my boy. You have to pick your battles. Most of them aren't worth the fight so you just have to learn to go with it."

"So, to be a good husband I have to eat shit for the rest of my life? Gee, can't wait," said Jim. "I wish someone would have told me that about marriage before I signed the papers. No offense, of course. Maye is my world, I mean …."

"No need to explain and no offence taken," Chuck interrupted, "we both know my daughter can be a lot to handle … but let me teach you a little something about marriage with a story about my day today. Will you indulge me, Son?"

Do I have a choice? thought Jim. "The floor is yours, Dadio." he said with lackluster enthusiasm.

"Thank you. If you bring your energy up a couple of notches when you pretend to be interested in what my daughter has to say, you'll be just fine," said Chuck. "You might only be half listening right now, but you'll hear what I'm talking about eventually. I didn't want to think about Evelynne today. After Sid and I had a few Gin Rickys with those Rockettes, Sid went home to the love of a good and beautiful woman."

"What did you do?" asked Jim.

"What else? I took Vera-Ellen and Adele back to my condo for a some wh …"

"Ope!" interrupted Jim. "Don't finish that. I get it."

"I've had a lot of wild liaisons trying to pass the time since Lynn died. I was a hot-shot salesman in the early eights; the woman came along too easily to pass up. Easy gets old, Jim. Easy gets old. Evelynne and I had our rough patches; especially while I was on the road a lot. I wasted quite a bit of our limited time together fighting over things that didn't matter. I wish I would've figured that out while I still had someone to fight with."

Chuck cleared his throat, holding back tears, "are you catching my drift, Son? he asked sternly.

"I think so."

"Good! Now, go put on your game face then put my daughter on the phone."

Page Break

Pete was sent next door while Jim took Maye to the emergency room. His impromptu visit to the Darlington house was met with mixed emotions.

"I suppose you'll be staying for supper, won't you Peter?" asked Lori with thinly veiled distain.

Pete sat to the left of Gwendoline at the piano in the dining room, pawing recklessly on the keys while she played "Heart and Soul." He was told to sit still and be patient until Gwendoline's piano lesson was finished, however, Pete was insistent he be able to "play piano" as well. Mrs. Teitelbaum, Lindinium's most sought-after piano instructor at the time, refused to continue Gwendoline's lesson amidst such nonsense. Gwendoline wasn't mad about it. She loved playing the piano for fun but hated practicing scales and proper finger technique under the tyrannical instruction of Tabitha Teitelbaum.

Pete kept playing as he looked back to answer Lori, "Yes, but I got my own dinner. I'm just going to eat it over here."

"I can't hear a word you're saying over all that racket you're making!" said Lori, covering her ears.

"I SAID I HAVE MY OWN FOOD!" He shouted, continuing to bang on the keys.

"Will you stop making noise for one moment, please! Gwendoline, you give it a rest as well."

"But we're in the middle of playing piano, Mrs. Darlington," said Pete.

"Yeah, Mom; we're playing piano." added Gwendoline. "Isn't that what it's for?"

"What just happened was not playing the piano; It was noise! Just noise! I did not pay top dollar for you to learn on a Kimball, Viennese edition, so you could make noise. Classic Piano is not a game."

"You mean *I* paid top dollar for a baby grand piano…." mumbled Dr. Darlington from behind his newspaper.

"What was that from the peanut gallery?" Lori asked her husband.

"Nothing, dear. Pete said he has his own dinner," he said, chortling awkwardly.

"I'll bet that's what you said, Phil. As for you, Peter … Is my food not good enough for you?" Lori asked, attempting to make a joke.

"Mom!" Gwendoline interjected.

"No Ma'am!" said Pete. "I mean, yes, ma'am; I love your food. It doesn't have a toy, though. I want a new Moon Man."

"What's a 'new Moon Man'?" Lori asked.

"I don't get my Happy Meal toy unless I eat all of my food! We were supposed to eat earlier but didn't," said Pete.

"What is the world coming to when parents don't have the authority to make their children eat without incentivizing it with a toy or reward?" Lori said.

Dr Darlington set down his paper, took a puff of his freshly packed tobacco pipe and blew a giant plume that engulfed the entire room with cherry flavored smoke. He rose from his favorite chair and walked slowly towards the piano, puffing away as he prepared himself for a monologue.

"It's not an incentive for kids to eat food; it's conditioning kids to want to eat the food at McDonald's. It's simple really," he said, leaning on the edge of the piano. "They give the kids toys in order to trick them into begging their parents to come back to McDonald's all the time. It's the same concept with their little Playland. Kids don't like McDonald's, they like what's associated with McDonald's: toys and fun. Grown-ups don't actually like McDonald's either. They just like that it's cheap and fast. Two dollars and twenty-five cents for a Big Mac that's already waiting for you when you order is too good of a deal to think about how bad it is for you."

"Thanks for the lesson in economics, Phillip." said Lori. "You should go back to teaching; I don't think you get to hear yourself talk enough anymore."

"I'm just shocked you even know what a Happy Meal is, Dad. *I've* never had one!" Gwendoline said.

"You should consider every meal that I provide, and which your mother cooks for you, a happy meal!" Dr. Darlington replied.

"Oh, because of the starving kids in Africa, Dad?" asked Gwendoline. "If I don't finish my meatloaf tonight, just call Sally Struthers so she can bring the leftovers with her next time she goes."

"I hope it's the Moon Man on a jet ski this time; I don't have that one yet," said Pete. "I'll go home and get it, after me and Wendy are done practicing piano."

"When *Gwendoline* and *I* finish practicing *the* piano," Lori said with emphasis on Pete's grammar.

"You and Wendy are going to practice, too?" Pete asked not picking up on Lori's corrective tone.

"What? No, never mind. Just go get your fish sandwich. We are going to eat soon." Lori said.

"That's silly, Lori," said Dr. Darlington. "We can't make the boy eat cold French fries, while we enjoy a hot meal, fresh from the oven, right in front of him."

"I suppose. Lord knows the boy isn't getting any hot meals next door." agreed Lori.

"No, my dad puts it in the microwave," said Pete. "It always has smoke coming out of the bun; that means it's hot and it's going to taste good."

"Reheated fast food hardly counts as a hot meal," Lori said bluntly. "Perhaps it wouldn't have to be microwaved if Jim didn't stop to do d-o-p-e in the driveway. You ought to have a talk with him, Phil."

"DOPE?" Gwendoline asked.

"Shhhh!" said Lori.

"Say nope to dope!" said Pete.

"That's very good, Pete." said Phil. "Like the candy guy on the Grape Heads box, right?"

Pete nodded confidently.

"Why don't you run next door and get your toy," suggested Dr. Darlington, "that way it'll be ready and waiting for you to play with after you clean your plate; okay?"

Pete scampered through the kitchen and out the back door, excitedly slamming it behind him.

"What is your problem, Lorraine?" asked Dr. Darlington. "He's a child; he needn't know about his father's d-r-u-g-s problem."

"Dad?" asked Gwendoline. "You realize I have the reading comprehension of a seventh grader, right? Mom didn't spell out the word *dope* for my benefit."

"It would benefit you to mind your own business, young lady!" Lori yelled. "Reefer madness or not, that child isn't our responsibility. I told you this would happen, Phil. They want to play 'house' when it's fun then send him on over to us when they need a break like we're his grandparents! First, they leave for the evening, then overnight. Soon enough, they'll be vacationing by themselves because they need a break. All the while, I'm running a flippin' day care! What am I supposed to do when I need a break?"

"They didn't go out dancing, Lori; Maye had to go to the emergency room for God's sake!"

"It's always something with that one. I wouldn't be surprised if she's faking it for attention, I told you we'd end up too involved in the neighbor's lives."

"If hindsight were nickels, we'd all be millionaires. Should Pete suffer because his parents haven't quite figured it out yet?"

"Of course not, Phillip," said Lori, "Gwendoline's future can suffer instead. Let's let her daydream and play her adolescence away until she grows up to marry a loser she can flounder through life with! I've worked too darn hard to keep her life pointed in the right direction to watch her veer off track and get lost in that boy's imagination. There are going to be some changes around here!"

Maye died of non-Hodgkin's lymphoma three months later. In her last season of life, she rarely left her bedroom. Pete was told she simply wasn't feeling well, and that Grampa Chuck had moved in with them to play more. Chuck commandeered the couch as well as the role of Maye's principle caretaker. Jim got as high as possible and worked as much as possible to keep himself in sustained denial.

"Another late night at the office, aye Jimbo?" said Chuck from Jim's favorite spot on the couch.

The Jolly Roger set sail for three dinner excursions per evening. Each service was timed meticulously from start to finish, however, the bar stayed open on the nights last voyage for as long as the customers were drinking. There was no telling when Jim might get off some nights, so he used his extra time for a few extra pokes of his pinchee at the edge of the driveway.

Chuck was waiting up for Jim as if he'd broken curfew. The living room was dark except for the light of the television. Chuck had his feet propped up across the length of the sofa with his back facing the door. He was paging through an old *TV Guide* as if he could read in the dark, and listening to the price of limited items drop dramatically – "for a short time only" -- on the QVC Home Shopping Network.

"Duty calls," Jim shrugged. "I thought everyone would be asleep by now. Sorry if my headlights woke you up."

"I was just doing some reading," said Chuck, slapping the magazine against his hand.

"In the dark?" Jim asked, flipping on the light switch by the front door.

"They're going to give the Tonight Show to the Doritos guy! Can you believe that? What's the world coming to?"

"Right," Jim said dismissively. "Is Maye sleeping?"

"Is she ever not?"

"A guy can hope. I guess I'll just lay down next to her and watch non-cable T.V. until I pass out," said Jim.

"Careful not to wake Pete up. He's in there sleeping too." said Chuck.

"Great." Jim said, rolling his eyes. He put his jacket back on and started for the front door.

"Where are you going?" Chuck asked, turning toward Jim.

"Nowhere. Gonna sit by the lake or something."

"Heavy emphasis on the *or something*," said Chuck, pretending to smoke a joint, "I'm not stupid, Cheech. What is it? You'd rather get stoned than hang out with your old-man-in-law? Have a seat, son."

Jim walked towards Chuck on the couch.

"Whoa, whoa. What's the ante Jimmy Durante?" asked Chuck. "I'm lying down, here. Go sit in the chair. What are you trying to neck with me or something, Jimbo?"

"Muscle memory I guess," shrugged Jim, "I'm used to my spot on the sofa."

"Nonsense," chuckled Chuck, "Everyone knows that king of the castle sits on the throne. For regular Joe's, or should I say Jim's and Chucky's like me and you, that throne is his comfy recliner, not his favorite *cushion*. The Sofa is for company. The Love seat is for loving, obviously … and the recliner always belongs to the man of the house.

"I'll try to remember that" said Jim, accepting defeat as he sat down in the Lazy Boy.

"Did you know the doctors told me I couldn't have children, Jim?" said Chuck, apropos of nothing.

"Is that so?" Jim asked, anticipating a long story to follow.

"Yes sir! Lynn and I tried for years to make a baby. Nothing! I was fine with it at first. I was always on the road and working anyhow. When the doc told me I couldn't make a child, it hit me in my manhood. I took pride in providing for my wife, but it felt like that was taken away from me. I built this castle for my queen from practically nothing; but nothing was all the kingdom was worth to her without our princess to inherit it one day."

"Not to take the piss out of your story, Dad, but doesn't your family own a city or something? That's not really starting with nothing."

"My family made their fortune in mining," Chuck said. "Sure, it may have laid the foundation for this house but since nothing but continuing the family business would have honored our family name enough in my parents' eyes, I stopped trying. And they cut me off. Fuck them, right? God rest their souls. This ain't half bad for a castle that curtain rings built."

"I see …. So how did Maye come along?" asked Jim.

"Pure miracle," said Chuck. "I've never been one for religion myself. I know a Ponzi scam when I see one. However, I've got to give the man upstairs his credit for my baby girl. I was staying at a Howard Johnson in Mankato. There was a home show that weekend, but they might as well have called it the Chuck Hookston Experience. Jim, I was on fucking fire that weekend. The star of the show. Not a soul left the River Hills Mall that Saturday without a new set of rings in their bag."

"Those were the days, huh?" Jim asked unenthusiastically.

"Anyways," said Chuck, "*Casablanca* was on TMC: It was our favorite film when we were young, Evelynne and me. I didn't usually call home over a short weekend trip, but I was on a real sales high and

Bogie had me missing my wife. What good is it to be the King of Rings without my queen by my side?"

"Naturally," said Jim.

"I called home to tell Evelynne I loved her, but the phone was off the hook. I don't know why but my first instincts told me she was having an affair. I drove ninety miles per hour all the way home."

"Was she cheating?" Jim asked, now actually interested in the story.

"Hell no!" proclaimed Chuck. "She didn't even know the phone was off the hook. When I got home, it was only her and Phil having tea."

Jim was hesitant to respond.

"But uhm … didn't you think that maybe Ph …

"I wasn't thinking at all, Son." interrupted Chuck. "Not about what was important. I'm just lucky that my Lynnie bear was turned on by my jealousy that night. We got it on, and nine months later, I was a daddy. I gave up life on the road and the glamor of selling rings for the insurance game so I could stay close to what was most important. I spent every second I could with Evelynne after I found out she was dying. After she passed and even to this day, I regret all the time I missed before that. Jim, all I'm saying is you might want to cherish what you have while you have it."

*****Page Break*****

Pete boarded the bus to ride home on his last day of school with his jacket tied around his waist, a backpack full of the swag he'd ordered from the Scholastic Book Fair, and a head full of anticipation and excitement for summer.

"Good afternoon, cadet," Davey said, saluting Pete as he daydreamed his way up the bus stairs. "Or should I say, Ensign Panneli."

Pete stopped abruptly just before the last stair to salute Davey, nearly causing the children lined up behind him to stumble forwards like dominos.

"Afternoon, Abneral Davey!" Pete said, then thought for a moment. "What's that?"

"Well … kindergarten is over for you so you're not a cadet anymore. You've earned a promotion in the ranks!" said Davey. "Congratulations! First grade is the big leagues!"

"Thanks!" said Pete. "Will I be a Abneral like you when I get to second grade?"

"It's *Admiral*, Ensign," Davey said. "You're going to need a lot more stripes to rise to my ranks. Go find your seat in the meantime; you're holding up the line again."

The innocuously curious nature of Pete's daily line of questions for Davey often came to the chagrin of his meticulous route schedule. He found himself getting sucked into Pete's imaginative riffs and banter increasingly as the school year progressed. Davey would try to be stern with Pete at times, but Pete thought it was all a part of the 'Navy' game they played together.

"Aye, aye, Admiral Ensign!" Pete said, saluting.

"No … it's … never mind, Pete. Go sit down, please."

Pete walked to his usual seat next to Gwendoline in the back of the bus.

"What did you get from the bookfair, Wendy?" Pete asked as he took his seat.

"The book fair is for babies. I don't get to pick which books I want to read over the summer: What's fair about that?" She said morosely.

"I don't know … but I got a bunch of stuff!" said Pete. "Re-erasers, this giant pencil, a slap bracelet, and I would have got the racecar poster, but my dad didn't have any birthday money left."

"Did you get any books from the book fair, Peter?"

"Duh," said Pete. "I was just telling you what I got for me. The books are for my mom. Reading me books always used to make her happy, but she never feels good enough to read to me anymore. New books should do the trick, I think."

Gwendoline was aware of Maye's prognosis but was instructed not to tell Pete.

"That's nice of you, Peter. What books did you get for your mom?"

"*Goodnight, Moon* and *Love You Forever*." he said proudly. "I can't wait to show her!"

Pete's glee plummeted as he entered a room full of somber faces. Maye died that morning shortly after Pete left for school.

Jim was sitting on the floor with his knees bent and his face resting in his palms. Chuck stood, staring out the window. Dr. Darlington was sitting at the dining room table with Lori, shaking his head solemnly while he held back tears and Lori stroked his tightly clenched fists to comfort him.

"What's the matter?" Pete asked with apprehension. "Why is everyone so sad?"

Everyone in the room looked to someone else to answer him.

"Peter, honey, come over here," said Lori.

Lori released her grasp of her husband and held her arms out towards Pete. As he walked toward her, scared and confused, Lori's eye's began to well up, already feeling the weight of Pete's impending grief. She swooped Pete into her arms from her chair before he could see a tear fall. Still struggling to formulate the right words, all Lori could do was breathe him in deeply and hug him with all of her might. She swayed from left to right, stroking his hair with a soft, downward motion. Pete began to weep, but he wasn't sure why.

"Please tell me why you're crying, Mrs. Darlington. It's making me cry!"

Jim arose from his crouched position on the living room floor with tears of hysteria, crying so hard he struggled to breathe and speak at the same time.

"Ma… May Maye's gone! Your Mom is gone, Pete!!"

"Gone? Where'd she go? She's coming back, right?" Pete said even more frightened and confused.

Jim rolled over to a fetal position and continued sobbing. Lori braced Pete by the shoulders.

"Your mother… well, she passed away, Peter. I'm so sorry, sweetheart; she was very, very sick, honey!"

"No, she wasn't!" Pete said angrily. "She was playing Hydrocoldasac! She was just tired! Did you check really good? She might be sleeping!"

Pete broke loose from Lori's grip and ran to the master bedroom to see for himself. The coroners had left hours ago, but her bed was still unmade, her pillow still creased from where her head lie.

Pete dropped to the floor in an inconsolable fit, rolling around, bellowing "I just got a Mommy!" and "It's not fair!"

Jim, Lori, and Dr. Darlington approached Pete as a unit to console him, but his little arms and legs flailed too wildly.

"I know it's not fair, buddy," consoled Jim, "We're all sad, but at least we are all sad together …"

"No!" shouted Pete. "None of your mommies just died! I want my Wendy!!"

Pete sprang up, wiggled through the legs of the adults, and ran out the back door. Dr. Darlington jogged after Pete and Jim continued to sob on the floor while Lori stood shaking her head sorrowfully.

"I hate that he calls her Wendy!" said Lori.

The End.

Pete & Gwendoline Will Continue to Grow in Season 2.

We did it, Grandma!

End Credits ...

Editor in Chief:

Rob K. Peach

Editorial advisory board:

Adam Herman

Kyle Scherz

Cover Art:

John Jason Phillips

Created by:

J.S. Thompson

Have a neat summer!

Follow Your Bliss ...

www.ingramcontent.com/pod-product-compliance
Lightning Source LLC
Chambersburg PA
CBHW060332310726
48976CB00007B/2535